Wataru Watari
Illustration Ponkan⑧
5
D0862060

Contents

MY YOUTH ROMANTIC COMEDY iS WRØNG, AS I EXPECTED

Wataru Watari
Illustration Ponkan⑧

VOLUME
5

NEW YORK

MY YOUTH ROMANTIC COMEDY IS WRONG, AS I EXPECTED Vol. 5
WATARU WATARI
Illustration by Ponkan⑧

Translation by Jennifer Ward
Cover art by Ponkan⑧

YAHARI ORE NO SEISHUN LOVE COME WA MACHIGATTEIRU.
Vol. 5 by Wataru WATARI

Original Japanese edition published by SHOGAKUKAN.
English translation rights arranged with SHOGAKUKAN through Tuttle-Mori Agency, Inc., Tokyo.

Yen On
1290 Avenue of the Americas
New York, NY 10104

Visit us at yenpress.com
facebook.com/yenpress
twitter.com/yenpress
yenpress.tumblr.com
instagram.com/yenpress

First Yen On Edition: May 2018

Yen On is an imprint of Yen Press, LLC.
The Yen On name and logo are trademarks of Yen Press, LLC.

The publisher is not responsible for websites (or their content) that are not owned by the publisher.

Library of Congress Cataloging-in-Publication Data
Names: Watari, Wataru, author. | Ponkan 8, illustrator.
Title: My youth romantic comedy is wrong, as I expected / Wataru Watari ; illustration by Ponkan 8.
Other titles: Yahari ore no seishun love come wa machigatteiru. English
Description: New York : Yen On, 2016–
Identifiers: LCCN 2016005816 | ISBN 9780316312295 (v. 1 : pbk.) | ISBN 9780316396011 (v. 2 : pbk.) | ISBN 9780316318068 (v. 3 : pbk.) | ISBN 9780316318075 (v. 4 : pbk.) | ISBN 9780316318082 (v. 5 : pbk.)
Subjects: | CYAC: Optimism—Fiction. | School—Fiction.
Classification: LCC PZ7.1.W396 My 2016 | DDC [Fic]—dc23
LC record available at http://lccn.loc.gov/2016005816

ISBN: 978-0-316-31808-2

10 9 8 7 6 5 4 3 2 1

LSC-C

Printed in the United States of America

Cast of Characters

Hachiman Hikigaya........... The main character. High school second-year. Twisted personality.

Yukino Yukinoshita........... Captain of the Service Club. Perfectionist.

Yui Yuigahama................... Hachiman's classmate. Tends to worry about what other people think.

Yoshiteru Zaimokuza......... Nerd. Ambition is to become a light novel author.

Saika Totsuka.................... In tennis club. Very cute. A boy, though.

Saki Kawasaki..................... Hachiman's classmate. Sort of a delinquent type.

Shizuka Hiratsuka............. Japanese teacher. Guidance counselor.

Komachi Hikigaya............. Hachiman's little sister. In middle school.

Taishi Kawasaki................. Saki Kawasaki's little brother. Goes to the same cram school as Komachi.

Haruno Yukinoshita........... Yukino's older sister. In university.

Kamakura........................... The Hikigaya family cat.

Sablé................................... The Yuigahama family dog.

MY

Summer Vacation Homework: Independent Research Project

The Mystery of Fireworks

Komachi Hikigaya

It's summertime, and that means fireworks!
You can see them all over Chiba.☆
In this report, I will delve into the mystery of fireworks!

1

◆What makes fireworks different colors?

★They burn different colors thanks to an effect called a flame reaction!

2

◆What's a flame reaction?

★A flame reaction is what
happens when the salts of alkali
metals or alkaline earth metals
such as copper are exposed to
flame. Each metallic element
burns with a distinctive color.
This is used both when doing
qualitative analysis of metals
and to color fireworks.
Apparently.
★Oh, but when my big brother
is with me, my world is always
colorful! Wow, that was worth a
lot of Komachi points!

3

◆Different types of flame reactions

★Below are some classic flame reactions~ ☆

- Lithium............crimson red
- Sodium............yellow
- Potassium.........lilac
- Calcium............orange
- Strontium.........scarlet red
- Barium............pale green
- Copper............bluish green

You'll also get color from
sodium chloride, otherwise
known as table salt. You can
buy salt at the convenience
store, so if you use your
card, you can rack up the
rewards! And that just now
was worth a lot of frequent
shopper points!

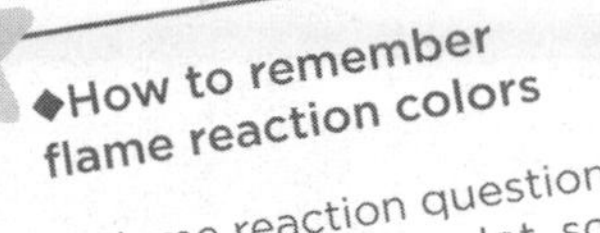

◆How to remember flame reaction colors

★Flame reaction questions show up on tests a lot, so let's make up a song about them to make the colors easy to remember! Now you'll never forget!

- Lithium (Li).........red
- Copper (Cu) ......green
- Barium (Ba).........green
- Iron (Fe)...............doesn't react

I don't ***li***ke ***re***ading, and I'm a ***cu***te ***ba***by grape~ ♪

"***Fwe***hhh...there's no flame reaction..." ♪

◆—IN-SUMMARY—◆

By observing flame reactions, you might be able to figure out the true identities of certain metals and substances! And if you look at it another way, fireworks, which use flame reactions, might help you learn what your crush really thinks and feels!

But generally, anyone who gets too excited during fireworks probably has a dirty mind, so maybe it's best not to know!

"Shoot out and mix together!"
Feh! Dirty old fireworks!"

1

All of a sudden, the tranquility of the **Hikigaya** household collapses.

Sprawled out atop the wooden floorboards, I clacked away on the laptop. The independent research project was almost done. I just had to format it, and it would be complete.

Not that the project was mine. My high school had only assigned me a measly few math problems, and I finished those off quickly enough just by copying down the answers. It's fine. I'm aiming for a private arts college; I don't need math.

Anyway, this project was for my little sister, Komachi.

As for the girl in question, she was curled up beside me to recoup her energy after studying for her high school entrance exams. She was playing with our cat, Kamakura, gently tossing him up like a baby and smooshing his toe beans and stuff.

Why you little… And I'm doing all this work for you… Why don't I smoosh your toe beans, too?!

Well, I did want her to focus on her entrance exams, so this one was on the house, at least. Common sense would dictate that such an assignment is pointless unless the assignee does it herself—and common sense would be right—but when it comes to my sister, conventional wisdom is obsolete.

Ethics and logic don't amount to much here: You write the character for "younger sister" by combining the radicals for "woman" and "not yet."

In other words, she is a woman whose future has just begun, and ultimately, she is also the last among her kin: She is the alpha and omega. She is the origin and yet the ultimate. You could even call her the final form of femininity. And her position as the pinnacle of womankind cements the little sister's rank as first or second among all living beings, and no way could I oppose one of those. And thus, I prove the theory of little sister supremacy.

Anyway, that was why I was responsible for the majority of Komachi's independent research project. ...*But really, why am I doing this? Oh, of course. Perhaps the art of using people and cultivating social connections for personal gain is also a part of her studies.*

These thoughts and others floated through my head as my fingers moved across the keyboard, finishing off the inane report on a pleasant note. *All right, now all I have to do is sign it with Komachi Hikigaya's name.* I gave the enter key a good *SLAM* to save the file and then pushed the whole laptop over toward Komachi.

"I finished your project. Be sure to check it over."

"Okay." Komachi rolled and lolled over the floor until she was beside me. She looked at the screen, bobbing her head with a periodic *mm-hmm, mm-hmm*, but then she froze mid-nod. "Bro," she began slowly. Her voice was lower in pitch than I'd ever heard it, but the grin on her face was terrifyingly radiant. "What is this?" she asked.

Her question triggered a primeval anxiety in me. "U-um...I was trying to make it Komachi-like...," I replied.

Her shoulders trembled. "Komachi-like? So this is what you think of me... I'm in shock! Total shock!" She groaned and clutched her head and started rolling around on the floor. It was cute enough that I watched her antics for a while, but then she leaped to her feet and jabbed an aggressive finger at me. "Wait, it's not Komachi-like at all, though! Those last two bits were all you!"

I see; so that was a no-go after all. Yeah, I had a feeling it wouldn't work. Wait, does that mean the first half was comparatively believable for Komachi? That's even more surprising. "Fine, I'll do it over," I said. "Just gotta get it done, right? Yeah, yeah, I'll take care of it. It's not even my job, but I'll shut up and do it."

"Hey! Don't give me that half-assed attitude! You sound like some low-ranking office drone!" Komachi was hopping mad, hands on her hips. But after a long-suffering sigh, she groaned with an apologetic expression. "…Well, it was my homework in the first place, so I'll take it from here. Thanks for doing this much."

Her good attitude about it made me wish I'd done a proper job, too. *No matter how annoying the project was, once I accepted it, maybe I should have done it properly*, I thought uncharacteristically. "Well, actually…," I said, "I kinda stopped caring at the end and just wrote whatever… I'm sorry, though. I'll do my best to help you."

The moment I said that, Komachi's eyes lit up like those of a *yamapikaryaa*. That's what we call Iriomote wildcats around here. *Yamapikaryaa!*

"I thought you would say that!" she exclaimed. "This is why I love you, Bro!"

"Yeah, yeah. I love, love, really love, super love you, too," I replied casually. Her usual Komachi points were exploding everywhere, and I was slightly fed up with it. Well, I had already done the research, so I could write the conclusion, at least.

As I gave her the rundown on the project, the cat padded over to us and apathetically plopped himself down in front of the monitor. Why do cats always stand in front of TVs and climb on top of newspapers?

"Komachi," I said.

"Roger!" She saluted and began executing her stratagem to relocate Kamakura. She seized him in her arms, and the cat wriggled in an attempt to escape. In Japanese, *cat hair* is an idiom that describes any fine, soft hair, and of course a real cat's hair is silky. But when Komachi swiftly began skritching his neck, he let his guard down and allowed her to continue into a full-on petting session. Utterly cheerful, Komachi hummed as she carefully stroked him from head to tail.

"Heh-heh-heh!" she chuckled. "What a bad little boy you are, coming to bother us! ☆"

"In cat years, he's already middle-aged, though." *What age is he again? It's been four or five years since we got him… Well, that's life. In human years, he'd probably be around Miss Hiratsuka's age. I should introduce them.*

Finally free to start on my own stuff, I handed the project materials to Komachi. The time was nearly eleven AM, and I had to get ready for my summer class in the afternoon. I got changed into whatever was closest, and that's when the doorbell rang. *Oh, is it Amazon coming again to deliver after they missed me the last time? It's uncanny how they show up whenever I'm not around. Like, are you ninjas or something?*

When I opened the front door all ready to sign for my package, I found an unexpected visitor.

"Y-yahallo!" With her bleached-brown bun, summery clothes, and a large carrier in both hands, Yui Yuigahama was idly yet self-consciously waiting.

"H-hey…," I replied. This was so unexpected, I didn't quite know how to respond. Neither did she, and an awkward silence ensued. The only people who ever came to our door were the delivery guy and the lady next door who drops off notices from the neighborhood association, so I couldn't believe that someone from school had actually stepped into my private domain. An analogy would be like seeing a gazelle at the aquarium. Gazelles are only supposed to show up on the savanna, at zoos, or in *Kinnikuman Nisei.*

Tightly grasping the open door, I feigned composure and asked, "Did you need something?"

This would be the second time Yuigahama had visited my house. The first time was after the traffic accident I've mentioned previously, when she came to say thank you. I didn't meet her in person back then, though.

"U-um…is Komachi here?" she asked.

My sister must have invited her over for something. "Komachi, dear! Your friend is here!" I called in my best mom-voice.

Komachi pitter-pattered down the stairs to us. Sometime since I'd seen her last, she had changed her entire outfit. *Weren't you wearing nothing but a T-shirt a second ago?*

"Yui, hello!" she said. "Come in, come in! Please, make yourself at home."

"Yeah, thanks! W-well. Sorry to intrude..." Despite announcing her intent to come in, though, Yuigahama seemed a little hesitant. She quietly took a breath as if to steel herself and then stepped up into the house. *Come on, it's not like it's a major dungeon.*

Once inside, Yuigahama glanced about curiously. *Stop that. You don't have to touch the wooden carved bear or anything.*

A stranger's house is a mystery zone, an outer zone, a twilight zone. You get culture shock when you enter another way of life, right? Yuigahama was taking in everything, even the totally ordinary stuff like the stairs, windows, and walls. With every glance, she mumbled "Huh..." or "Whoa..." It was mildly irritating.

Even after she was escorted to the living room on the second floor, she did not settle down, and her gaze darted all over. But when it hit the bookshelf, she stopped and stared at it. She slid her finger along the surface, a little taken aback. "Whoa, it's stacked with books."

"My dad and brother both like reading, so we're always collecting more," Komachi replied from the kitchen counter.

I didn't feel like we had so many, but Yuigahama didn't exactly strike me as a bibliophile...

It's extremely rare for a guest to visit our house. Our family is as modern as it gets: Both our parents work, so we don't really get to know anyone nearby. When I run into the neighbors on the street, I'll give them a bow, at least, but I know basically nothing about them beyond their names.

Which means I have no idea what the protocol is when you have a guest. I guess I'm nothing but a rude and brash fool. I might even end up spilling ashes all over the mortuary tablet at my dad's funeral. Aw, shucks, that makes me sound like some major historical figure. This is totally irrelevant, but people who get all self-important and start going on about how "Edison got bad grades in school!" never seem to have any other skills, either. The more you know.

I pulled out a chair and offered it to Yuigahama to silently suggest *Why don't you take a seat?* I'm not used to this, so I can't help being terse. I'm like some boy from the sticks handing an umbrella to a city girl in the middle of the rain. I might even follow it up with "Haven't you heard? You're living in a haunted house!"

"Th-thanks." Yuigahama gracefully sat down, and Komachi came back from the kitchen, setting a cup on the table before her with a tap. The ice in the barley tea clinked.

"So, what are you here for?" I asked. I had no idea why Yuigahama would come here.

Yuigahama indicated the large carrier she clasped carefully on her lap. "Um, it's about Sablé. I asked Komachi to help me out with him," she said, and then she opened the box.

A creature of indescribable and profane fuzziness leaped out, crawling in my direction, its chaos embodied in brown fur, round eyes, short legs, and a little waggy tail. In another age, it would have been the most noble of animals: the dog.

Yuigahama's pet, Sablé, locked onto me and hurtled forward. Am I Frisky Mon Petit or what? The dog was booking it straight for me with everything he had, and he did not stop.

Sablé uses Tackle! It's super effective! Hachiman fainted!

He knocked me down hard, and I peeled the dog off as he continued slobbering all over me. I raised him up, but I could see his tail was still vigorously wiggling.

"What's with this dog?" I asked. "Wait. Has its fur gotten shorter?" I got the impression he'd gotten one size smaller since I'd seen him two months ago. Had he been using the Beast Spear, then, or something?

"Oh yeah," said Yuigahama. "Sablé is long-haired, so we got him a summer cut."

"Uh-huh..." Well, he can get a somersault or an uppercut or a spinning pile driver if he wants. "So why'd you bring your doggy here?"

Even after I released Sablé, he wheeled around and around my ankles, refusing to go away. He was so stubborn, I didn't know what to do. *Woof, woof, wa-woof.* I shot Yuigahama a look that pleaded, *Come on, do something.*

"Sablé, come here," she called to him, and when he went over to her, she scooped him up and began gently petting him as she continued speaking. "My family is going on a vacation together."

A family vacation, huh...? There's a term loaded with nostalgia. I never thought I'd hear about those in high school, but I suppose I didn't have anyone to talk to about it in the first place, anyway, no, sir. "Your family sounds close," I said. "Not like us."

"You're the one getting left behind, Bro," Komachi said without missing a beat.

Yuigahama shivered. "I'd expect nothing less from you, Hikki...," she muttered. The way she put it, it sounded almost respectful. *Whoa, maybe she has an eye for people,* I thought, but nope, her eyes were just pitying me.

"That's not true," I protested. "This one time in middle school, I said I wasn't going, and then, well, they just never took me after that." I hadn't been going through a rebellious phase or anything. It just felt oddly embarrassing to go on a trip with my family. That's why I said no. But the old man was freaking thrilled... Well, never mind my dad. We're talking about Yuigahama's vacation. "So what about this trip of yours?" I asked.

"Oh yeah," she said. "While we're away, I was hoping you guys could take care of Sablé." Eyes upturned, she asked me, "No?"

I am The Japanese That Can Say No: capable of refusing most requests. But confronted with Komachi's beaming smile as she petted Sablé, I found it hard to turn Yuigahama down.

Still, I couldn't just obediently comply with her demands and hand her an instant yes. There are no instant answers in life.

"...You don't have to take him all the way out here, though. We're pretty far." *I'm sure she's got lots of friends, and I hear these days you can find pet hotels all over.*

"Yumiko's never had a pet, and neither has Hina. I tried asking

I
HIBA

Yukinon, but she said she can't really do it because she's at her parents' house..." Yuigahama faltered for a moment, looking uneasy.

Well, Yukinoshita is scared of dogs, so even if she weren't at her parents' house, I doubt she would've agreed to do it... No, maybe she actually would've been like, "Leave it to me!" and then oh-so-timidly offered him food.

As I entertained myself with these pleasant mental images, Komachi noticed Yuigahama's sudden silence and urged the other girl to continue. "Has something happened with Yukino?" she asked.

Yuigahama hesitated before uncertainly looking my way. "Y-yeah... Hikki, have you been in touch with her?"

"No, I don't even know her number." I don't have a messenger pigeon, so unless I put a letter in a bottle and set it adrift on the waves, I would have no way of getting a hold of her. I silently asked Komachi, *What about you?* But she shook her head.

"I e-mail and call her a lot, though," said Yuigahama.

"Did something happen?" I asked.

"When I call her, I get her voice mail, and then she'll send me an e-mail after. She takes a long time to reply...and when she does, it's like, it just seems halfhearted? When I invite her to hang out, she always has plans..."

"Uh-huh..." *Look, she's avoiding you. I mean, that's basically just how the kids in my class reacted back in middle school when I tried to keep in touch.* Or so I wanted to say, but I decided against it. Yuigahama had obviously already realized that Yukinoshita was trying to push her away. She's so good at reading people and blending in, there's no way she wouldn't figure out the most basic tells.

"I wonder if I did something...?" She laughed weakly.

"Don't stress over it too much. She might just have a lot on her plate, dealing with her family. When school starts again, I'm sure things will just work themselves out." It was an uncharacteristically encouraging thing for me to say. I'm good at spouting offhand, unsubstantiated remarks. It's like that old saying, "He's full of eight hundred lies." Except with me, it's eighty thousand. 'Cause I'm Hachiman. They should make that a thing.

Well, that wasn't necessarily a total lie. Things did look rough with Yukinoshita's family. There was that little episode around two weeks prior, at the beginning of August. We had all been saying our farewells after the camping trip, when Haruno Yukinoshita, her older sister, came to take her back home. None of us had seen the younger sister since then. And I was still having flashbacks about that black limo that drove off with them.

There had been a car accident one year ago involving me and Yuigahama...and the one responsible was in a black limo. I didn't know if that vehicle and the one we'd seen two weeks ago were one and the same. All that connected the two cars was my hazy memory. I had no proof of anything. There were no testimonies, no statements, no explanations, nothing.

A few humorless moments passed. Even after my half-assed attempt at encouragement, Yuigahama's worries hadn't subsided. "I—I guess..."

"Not that I have any idea," I said.

"Why do you have to be like that? You're so apathetic." Yuigahama gave me an exasperated smile.

I really don't know, though. I don't know Yukino Yukinoshita. Of course, I know about her on a superficial level. I know her name, her face, that she has good grades, that she keeps people at a distance, that she likes cats and Grue-bear, that she has a sharp tongue, and that she can be a little absentminded. But that's how it is. You can't act like you know someone based off that alone. Just as no one understands me, neither do I understand them. You can't forget that.

And what does it take to be able to say you "know" someone, anyway?

As I descended into a maze of contemplation, I heard some shrill little yips. When I turned to investigate the initial cry, a low, rumbling noise soon followed. Sablé and Kamakura were running in circles around Komachi, engaged in a contest of intimidation. Kamakura had his Get-Away-from-Me Barrier up, but Sablé destroyed it with a Love-Love-Kamakura Beam and gave chase. Komachi, smiling and amused as she watched them, did not make any particular attempt to stop them.

So I'm gonna have to deal with this for a while now, huh…?

Yuigahama must have picked up on my chagrin. "S-sorry. I thought about taking him to a pet hotel, but it's holiday season, so they're all filled up," she said apologetically with a laugh.

"And that's where I come in, Bro." *Thump!* Komachi gave a smug chuckle and arrogantly whacked a fist against her small chest with gusto. *Why are you acting so weirdly dependable? Are you the ship captain or what?*

Sigh. Well, it sounded like she e-mailed Yuigahama a lot, so it probably just came up during their conversation.

"If we don't do this now, we won't have any opportunities all summer. Chance," Komachi muttered quietly. I suspect her eyes may have sparkled ☆ there, but I was more distracted by her use of Zaimokuza's verbal tic, *chance. Has the virus spread from me to others? I don't want it to become a thing… Total sacrifice.*

"Well, if you don't mind, then whatever," I said. This was my shrewd little sister here. She'd probably already dealt with our mother. If she'd already defeated Mom, then the only remaining obstacle was our dad, and he was putty in her hands. In the Hikigaya household, the eldest son has no part in the decision-making process. There is a perfect hierarchy in place, and it goes Mom, Komachi, the old man, and finally, me. Oh, and of course, His Highness the Cat is up at the very top. To him, humans are but pawns.

"Anyway, we can take care of him or whatever, but what should we feed him?" I asked. "Vita-One? Frontline? Whoa, not Pedigree, right? We're not that fancy, you know."

"Why do you know so much about dog food?" Yuigahama asked. "Wait… Frontline is flea treatment! I dunno about this…" She seemed to be rethinking her decision, if her worried expression was any indication.

Komachi smiled, attempting to placate her. "It's okay! He used to have a dog."

"Y-you did?" asked Yuigahama.

"Sort of," I replied. It was a long time ago, though. My memories were vague. Actually, I think it was mostly my parents and Komachi who cared for it.

A hint of warmth crept into Yuigahama's smile. "Wow. I'm kinda surprised."

"My brother likes cats and dogs. It's just people he hates..."

Am I a certain former spirit detective now...?

Well, she's not wrong. I don't hate cats or dogs. I suppose they would even fall under the category of things I like. Especially cats.

Friends, I like cats. No, friends, I love cats! I love American shorthairs. I love tortoiseshells. I love sphynxes. I love Ragdolls and American curls; I love Scottish folds and Persians; I love Singapuras and Russian blues. Cats in alleys, in little cat huts, on cat towers, on top of fridges, on beds, on veranda railings, in cardboard boxes, in paper bags, on people's backs, on futons—I love every single cat that lives upon this earth.

You know, abuse of animals is unforgivable to me. People who don't cherish living beings can go and die. I hate anyone who doesn't value life!

As I composed impassioned speeches in my head, Yuigahama abruptly let a smile slip. "Well, that's a relief. It looks like Sablé likes you, too."

"Don't expect too much. I'm better at being taken care of than doing the caring. You could even call me a professional dependent," I replied.

I've been a dependent for seventeen years now. I can't think of any other way to live. Once you've spent your formative years relying on others, there's no going back. I ruffled Sablé's fur as he showed off his tummy and lolled around on his back beside me. But Komachi snatched him away.

"Well, you leave Sabby to me! It won't be long before he can't live without me!" Komachi was fully intent on seducing this dog away.

"I don't really want that, but... Okay, well, I'm leaving him to you." Despite her obvious apprehension, Yuigahama gave a quick bow, and her eyes darted to the inside of her wrist to check the time. "Oh, I have to get going. My parents are waiting."

"All righty, then," said Komachi. "I'll see you off."

Watching them out of the corner of my eye as they went down the stairs, I fished around in the carrier Yuigahama had left us. There was dog food inside, plus everything else we'd need to take care of him.

By the way, he eats Science Diet. His lifestyle is healthier than mine…

As for the canine in question, he was prowling and snuffling around the room. *Oh, guess he smells the cat.* As for Kamakura, he had apparently escaped the dog and was now on top of the refrigerator, gazing down on me and Sablé with languid eyes. I doubt he hated Sablé or even had much interest in him at all. He just kept his distance, kept alert, because he didn't know to approach the other animal. That faintly reserved gaze was familiar to me.

It had been Yuigahama's birthday, so I remembered it well.

It was a rare clear day during the rainy season. Silhouetted by a sunset red as guilt, she had smiled sadly. She drew a definite line then, I know.

It meant that we, the victims, were not like her.

Only now was I finally beginning to understand what that boundary was.

Hachiman's mobile

FROM Hachiman 19:45
TITLE Re
Nothing much is gonna change in a day.
You're being overprotective

FROM Hachiman 19:50
TITLE Re3
I told you, I just don't use them. Anyway, what am I supposed to do with this dog? Is there anything I should be watching out for? I need to know his long suits and where he comes up short, or I won't know how to deal with him

FROM Hachiman 19:55
TITLE Re5
Bye

FROM Hachiman 19:58
TITLE Re7
So where does he come up short?

FROM Hachiman 20:00
TITLE Re9
Moron ^ ^

Hachiman and Yui's mobile chat one day

Yui's mobile

FROM ☆★ Yui ★☆: 19:23
TITLE None
▽・W・▽ good doggy-vening! is sablé doing ok?

FROM ☆★ Yui ★☆: 19:48
TITLE Re2
srsly, u sound mad when u don't use emotes
(` ・ω・ ´)

FROM ☆★ Yui ★☆: 19:55
TITLE Re4
long? like…his torso (´ ・ω・`) ?

FROM ☆★ Yui ★☆:
TITLE Re6
wait wait! 4get i said that! Σ(° д °|||)

FROM ☆★ Yui ★☆:
TITLE Re8
his legs! (｡'ω'｡)

FROM ☆★ Yui ★☆: 20:01
TITLE Re10
that emote ticks me off! (* ` ω ´)

2

Sure enough, he's forgotten **Saki Kawasaki**.

It was early afternoon during summer vacation, and the train was less crowded than usual. I rode past a few stations to Tsudanuma and passed through the ticket gates, turned right, and joined the sparse current of people moving forward.

At the Tsudanuma campus of Sasaki Seminar, they held a summer course for second-year high schoolers. Most students thinking about entrance exams would already have begun preparing for them around then. Still, we were only second-years, so the mood was fairly relaxed. Once you hit third year, things get tense. If you fall asleep in class, they might even kick you out of the room. And after that, they take you to this little reception area where the lecturer goes off at you and the tutor is like, "...Will you switch lectures?" and you can tell they're scolding you. Or so I've heard on the Internet.

This particular class was for high school second-years aiming for selective private universities. The room was deserted.

Each course was five days long. English and Japanese were combined into one five-day course, and there was another optional five-day course for social studies. I had already finished social studies a little while ago, and now I was starting on English/Japanese.

When I entered the room, I didn't notice anyone there, so I took up my position in the front row, closest to the door. As a rule, the desks in the back are the VIP seats, so to speak. The prevailing wisdom is that the biggest clique will occupy them. Any involvement with them invites great suffering, so I always go with the front row or the exact center of the class. Even in the front row, the rightmost and leftmost seats are often blind spots, so that's where a loner should set his sights. Though it is a little hard to see the blackboard from there, it's easier to concentrate in class. I mean, since nobody comes to talk to you, you're inevitably forced to concentrate. In fact, it ends up being a decent spot.

I immediately set out my textbook and notebook and rested my face on my hand for some light zoning out before the start of the lecture. Watching the others pleasantly chatter away with their friends, I patiently waited for the appointed time.

This tranquility would probably be gone by this time next year. It had been like that during entrance exams for high school, too. People were secretly talking smack about anyone who had already gotten a recommendation and secretly cursing the people who were going to pass. I was certain that in our final year, it would just be the same thing. Four years after that, it would happen again when we started job seeking. Three years, seven years may pass, but I doubt the true nature of man will ever change.

But let's leave the past for now. What I needed to be focusing on were the things in front of me. First of all, the university entrance exams. Early birds would be shifting their focus toward college admissions this summer. It was time to pull that mental switch. My goal for now was the Center Test. Position the Center as target and pull the switch… Position the Center as target and pull the switch… Position the Center as target and pull the switch…

As I simulated the entrance exam mentality with hollow eyes, I caught sight of someone in my periphery, and I came to my senses. It was as if someone had yelled at me, *Idiot! You hid the enemy with your own smoke!*

Her waist-length, blue-tinged black hair was tied up in a ponytail, and her long, lithe legs drew the eye. She wore a shirt with three-quarter sleeves and denim shorts over leggings, and she had

a backpack slung loosely over one shoulder. Her sandals dragged over the ground with her languid stride as she passed by me and then stopped. Something about the pause was unnatural, so I looked at her.

"So you're in this class, too," she said in a sleepy-sounding voice as she threw me a chilly glance. Below one of her ill-humored eyes was a mole like a teardrop.

I feel like she looks familiar. Who is she again?

"I should thank you, though. I'm grateful," she continued.

I had no idea why she was thanking me, but nothing indicated she had the wrong person. It's very rare for someone to speak to a loner. Usually, it doesn't happen except in the most extreme of circumstances.

"Thanks to you, I got that...*scholarship*?" She fumbled over the English word. "One of those. Things are going well with Taishi, too."

The name Taishi sounded unpleasantly familiar. I consulted my list of people I hate and landed on the name Taishi Kawasaki. *Oh-ho, that's the little cockroach that tried to sidle up to Komachi.* What was his relationship to this person?

And then, thanks to her bluish-black hair, I suddenly recognized her. Blood Type Blue! Kawa... Kawakoshi? Kawajima? Kawaharagi...? Well, whatever. It's Kawa-something! Her hair was so blue, I thought she was a Gagaga book.

"Naw, you got that scholarship on your own," I replied. As we conversed, I remembered her name: Saki Kawasaki.

"Yeah, but Taishi keeps going on about you, so... Well, whatever, I've said it." That was all she said, as if motivated by a sense of obligation, and then immediately marched away. She was curt, but that was nothing new. Kawasaki doesn't let people get near, always chooses solitude, and exudes the air of a delinquent. And she had initiated the conversation with me.

I felt like she'd softened up quite a bit. Curious about her transformation, my eyes automatically followed her. She took a seat about three rows behind me and pulled out her phone. From the way her fingers were moving, she was probably writing an e-mail. And then she happened to smile.

Huh, so she *can* smile. She always looks so bored, and her presence is aggressively overbearing. You'd never see her smile like that at school. Actually, I don't recall seeing her at school too much in the first place. Among fellow loners, nonintervention is standard.

While I was watching her, thinking, *Huh, what a rare sight to see*, our eyes met. Blushing bright red, Kawasaki gave me an intense glare. *Eek! She's so scary!* I rolled my head like, *Man, my shoulders are so stiff!* and tried my best to escape. Nope, she hadn't softened up at all. You went to all that trouble to come to prep school, Kawasaki, so try to sand down those sharp corners. Make your square head round.

X X X

The English lecture ended, and it was our very brief break period. I headed downstairs and bought a MAX Coffee from the vending machine. Slowly sipping it, I returned to the classroom. Inside, the other kids were spending the time as they pleased—fiddling with their phones, reading, or having staring contests with the modern Japanese textbook for the next class. It was unlike what you'd normally see at school. Overall, a lot of people were by themselves; loners accounted for the majority.

It was a peculiar situation compared with the cram school I had attended the last time I had entrance exams. That had ultimately just been an extension of regular school. Even at these extra classes, the people who never fit in were still ignored in force. During lectures, that same social dynamic was in place. It was exasperating. That class had made me desperate to move on to the upper level. With each move up, the classroom got quieter, and the level of the lectures and the proficiency of the students increased.

Thinking back on it, maybe those lower-level students had just been looking for justifications to be satisfied with the basic classes, so they had flocked together. They turned their friendships into a reason to give up trying, their relationships into an excuse for complacency. It's like when a middle school couple says they want to go on to the same high school, and the smarter one goes to a less competitive school that's on their SO's level. At the time, when I had overheard people suggesting it, I had felt a chill. If you really want what's best for your girlfriend or boyfriend, you shouldn't hold them back or follow their every whim. That's just taking the easy route so they can continue to indulge in their idle and mundane lives.

Eventually, you'll hear through the grapevine that they did go to the same high school and broke up in less than two months. That's absurd. It's such a riot, you're bound to end up with smashed windows. And then they'll try to validate it later by going on about how they were sooo young back then, you know?

Maybe it's because I've watched it happen from an outsider's perspective, but I could never believe in any relationship that's so utterly superficial. It's a convenient excuse, and I don't trust any form of kindness so filled with deceit and so delighted in its own self-sacrifice.

That's why I liked this prep school system. The school maintained an appropriate policy of nonintervention with the students, and the students were all indifferent to one another. They completely did away with any process unnecessary for exam prep. It was fair to say that their goal was maximum efficiency.

At the cram school I went to in middle school, the lecturer and the students were all trying to be friends or something. It sucked… All the other students were on a first-name basis, and I was the only one they all called by last name…

I mean, if students and teachers want to be all buddy-buddy at prep school, it's doable. They've got this tutor system—basically, university students are always working part-time. Apparently, they don't just help you with your studies, they'll also talk to you about your career path. If you want to take part in a poignant student-teacher drama during your entrance exams, you're perfectly free to do so.

Fundamentally, the atmosphere around here is sound and serene.

Some might find it cold. For me, it's comfortable. Still, some of my classmates were of Hayama's breed. The way they blathered on to each other at high volume until the class started, it was like someone had urged them to "bring all your friends!"

You can find normie(LOL)-ish people everywhere you go. If you made a distribution map of their habitat, the sprawl would most certainly rival that of potato bugs or wharf roaches. I can't understand why anyone would want to be so mundane.

Good grief, the swarm is everywhere… And they're more active in summer. That's another way they're like insects. I hate bugs, so this season is always a struggle.

X X X

When the lecture was over, I was overcome with the characteristic lethargy that testifies to ninety minutes of continuous concentration. The fatigue of studying is unlike the comfortable exhaustion of playing sports. It feels like your head is gradually fogging over. The glucose in my brain was all used up. If I hadn't had that MAX Coffee, things might have taken a turn for the worse. TONE Coca-Cola Bottling should team up with somebody to make a product for exam takers. They'd probably make good money.

Having finished the lectures, I immediately began packing up to go home. This is when the loner is most cheerful.

Fortunately, the Tsudanuma area around the cram school was a fairly developed amusement district, so there were a number of bookstores and a lot of arcades. It was a neighborhood that could keep a high school boy entertained.

As I was considering whether I should make any stops on my way home, a *rap, rap* sounded on the edge of my desk. When I looked toward the cause, I found a sullen Saki Kawasaki. *What? If you have business with me, say something. Are your parents woodpeckers?*

"Do you need something?" I asked. She had been sending *Ask me!* vibes, so I obediently went along with it.

Kawasaki briefly hesitated, sighing.

Come on, if you don't want to talk to me, then don't. What do you want?

"Hey, do you have some time now?" she asked.

"Oh, I have a thing, so." I unconsciously activated my standard refusal line. I automatically react to these things; it's my instinct to refuse all invitations. It's a commonsense behavior in modern society, just like screening any call from an unknown number. When I use that line, in most cases, people will back down easily. *Oh, really? Okay...right.* Although the lack of resistance really gives the impression that they were only asking to be polite. In fact, sometimes they even imply that they're relieved you said no. Seriously, you guys, take more care with that. In my opinion, sometimes you have to be kind by withholding the invitation.

But I don't think Saki Kawasaki was speaking to me out of politeness. In fact, I got the impression that she didn't engage with that kind of etiquette. Her type doesn't back down, not even before Yukinoshita or Miss Hiratsuka. She pretty much says what she wants.

Kawasaki's languid eyes narrowed sharply. "What 'thing'?"

"Well, uh, like, *a thing*... Just some, like, stuff with my sister." In desperation, I appealed to Komachi.

Kawasaki gave me a small nod. "I see. That works out perfectly, then. Come with me for a bit."

"Huh?"

With great exasperation, Kawasaki answered my monosyllabic request for more information. "I'm not the one who wants to talk to you. Taishi says he wants to ask you something. He says she's with him in Tsudanuma."

Oh, I see. So that e-mail she was writing was to her brother. So did that little grin midtext mean she has a brother complex or something? *Hey, brah, how ya doin'?* Yeah, I could see her having a complex about her bra. My flat-chested sister says it's hard to find cute ones in the larger sizes.

"Sorry, but there's no reason for me to spend my time on your little brother."

"I'm saying your sister is with him, though."

"Hey, so where are we going, then? Is it close by? Five minutes' walk? Can we run?" *Tell me these things first, geez.*

"Seriously...?" She fired an exasperated glare my way.

But I didn't pay her any mind as I leaped to my feet and zoomed out of the classroom.

Kawasaki followed after me. "They're at the Saize right past the exit. Do you know where it is?" she asked.

"Please. I know where every Saize along the Sobu Line is located." I even know the former site of the first branch. Motoyawata is the birthplace of Saize. The shop is no longer there, but the sign is. By the way, I'm so informed about the area, I can even add that the head office and distribution center for Tora no Ana are also around Motoyawata.

When we left the building, a suffocating heat was hovering over the road. There was no wind, and it was like the humidity was bending the sunlight as it blazed down on us. It was in between lectures, and as we merged with the ebb and flow of people around the station, the population density of the neighborhood took a sudden upturn. We didn't talk much as we weaved ahead through the periodic gaps between the human waves. I'm almost always on my own when I'm out, so I'm good at slipping into the vacuums of the crowd as I walk. From here on out, the game will belong to Stealth Hikki, yo!

Komachi and the cockroach were apparently at a nearby Saize. Perfect. They have knives and forks there, so no lack of murder weapons. I could also pie-throw a piping-hot Milan-style cheesy pilaf right in his face. Then I'd just have to put up some on-screen text to reassure everyone that **the staff ate it all afterward!* All would be forgiven. And then I'd daub his wounds with spicy chicken sauce.

I could actually feel my soul gem darkening. *Whoops, that's not good. At this rate, I'll turn into a witch. Let's think about something nice... Is* Magical Girl Saika ☆ Totsuka *out yet?*

Fighting down my impatience, I waited for the traffic light to turn. Behind me, Kawasaki commented, "Oh yeah. A little while ago, Yukinoshita was taking a summer class, too."

"...Huh. Really?" The name delayed my reaction a little. I'm pretty sure Yukinoshita is aiming to go to a public sciences school. *So Kawasaki's taking those courses, too?* Well, it's natural to have a broad range of school choices at this point. I'm just narrowing my goal to a private arts school because I'm so dismal at math. By the way, I'm also narrowing my goal for the future to being a househusband.

"She really is hard to approach," Kawasaki commented.

Are you in a position to be saying that? You're constantly emitting a terrifying aura. Never mind the girls—half the boys are scared of you, too, you know?

"What's with that look?" Her listless eyes narrowed and flicked toward me.

"Nothing." Flustered, I turned away.

I could imagine what Yukinoshita and Kawasaki would be like together in the same classroom. Though both of them would attract a lot of attention, I bet neither let anyone get close. Their behavior is similar, but I think their motivations are completely different.

Behind Kawasaki's aggression is a failure to communicate. It's the quintessential tendency of the taciturn. I suspect she's just bad at talking. Seeing her affection for her little brother, you somehow know.

Yukinoshita, on the other hand, has never had any desire to go on the attack at all—her existence itself is an onslaught. Individuals who excel can be overwhelming, awakening jealousy and a sense of inferiority in others. That's what has cut her off from those around her and earned her their ill will. And then to complicate matters, she never fails to push back against the malice. She crushes it. That's Yukinoshita. If Kawasaki's behavior is a threat for the sake of self-defense, then Yukinoshita's behavior is always absolute retribution.

The light changed to green. When I took a step out, Kawasaki ventured, "Hey...could you thank her for me? In the end, I never did."

"Do it yourself."

"I could, I guess. But, well, I dunno... It'd be a little awkward." Her timidity caught my attention, so I looked at her. Her eyes were quietly downcast, and she was walking with her head lowered. "Some people you're just not going to get along with, even if you know they didn't do anything wrong," she said.

"Yeah." That's true. That's why noninterference is the best form of compromise. You can choose to stay out of it for the sake of getting by. Sticking together like glue and smiling and chatting and fooling around and hanging out are not the only possible ways to engage with people. I believe that keeping an appropriate distance in order to avoid hating one another is also laudable.

That's the impression Yukino Yukinoshita left on Saki Kawasaki. Kawasaki was forced to acknowledge her but could not approach. Kawasaki knew that nothing good would come of it if either of them attempted to reach out. She could be certain the pain they would inflict on each other would serve no purpose, and that's why she tried to avoid contact. It's not running away or sidestepping the issue: It's an indication of respect.

"Besides, we probably won't run into each other for a while," she said. "She's not in this course, so the next time I'll see her is at school, and we're not in the same class. But you'll see her again soon for your club activities, right?"

"No, I don't think I'll see her until school starts again, either." At the very least, we wouldn't be seeing each other on purpose. If you thought about it, that was all there was to our relationship. We wouldn't make contact unless we had to. I didn't even know her number.

We crossed to the other side of the crosswalk and went down a flight of stairs to the basement of the building. Our footsteps echoed quietly.

"Plus, even if we did run into each other, we wouldn't necessarily talk," I said.

"That's true. I don't normally talk to her, either."

"Yup." I mean, if someone starts a conversation with me, I'll give them a proper response. In fact, I'm extremely polite when I engage with people. So polite I come off as creepy. If I know someone is a loner, like Kawasaki, then I can relax and be more casual because I recognize we're of the same breed, I guess.

As we conversed, we reached the basement floor. When we passed through the automatic doors, I saw Komachi nearby in a seat close to the drink bar. As soon as she saw me, she waved her hand. "'Sup, Bro!"

"'Sup," I replied casually, plopping down beside her.

Across from her was a middle schooler with a name reminiscent of Sano Yakuyoke Daishi. When his eyes met with mine, he bobbed his head in a bow. "Bro! Sorry for making you come all this way."

"Don't call me Bro. I'll kill you."

"Hey. Are you trying to start a fight with my little brother?" Waves of rage were rolling off quiet Kawasaki in her seat opposite mine.

She's really glaring at me! These brother-complex types are seriously creepy. People who get overly attached to their family members freak me *out*. Seriously, dude.

Taishi was busy restraining Kawasaki as she attempted to intimidate me with a growl, so I dinged the bell and quickly took care of ordering.

Two more people for the drink bar. I was too scared of Kawasaki to smash a Milan-style cheesy pilaf in her face, so I gave up on that.

I picked up my cup of joe, as they say in the business, had a sip, and then got down to brass tacks. "So what do you want?" I asked.

"Oh yeah," Taishi replied. "I want you to tell me about Soubu High."

"Come on. Just ask your sister. She's right there," I said. Saki Kawasaki was in my year at the same school as me. I'd probably forget if I didn't remind myself.

"I really want another guy's opinion!" For some reason, Taishi was clenching his fists tight. *Why is he so worked up…?* He can be as passionate as he likes, but he's not going to get much out of me.

"It's not really anything special," I said. "I think any school would be about the same. Some of the special events might be different, depending on things like how serious they get with the cultural festival and how good the sports teams are." I've never seen any other high schools, so I don't know exactly, but that's my impression. If we're just talking about the regular curriculum in the full-day school system, you could probably fit most schools into the same stereotypical category. Unique programs aside, there's not such a huge difference between them. Personally, my naive mental image of high school and the reality of what it actually ended up being were virtually equivalent. My sole miscalculation was joining the Service Club under duress.

"Huh?" Komachi tilted her head curiously. "But when the school test-score averages are different, doesn't that change the school spirit?"

Well," I replied, "I think as the averages go up, you tend to find fewer delinquent types. Still, some people want to act like delinquents." I casually slid my eyes over to the spot diagonal from me.

Noticing my gaze, Kawasaki glared at me. "Why're you looking at me?" she asked. "I'm not trying to be a delinquent."

So my assumption had been off. Something had convinced me she was about to say, *Stop looking at my face. Look at my body. Come on.* So my eyes just…

I cleared my throat in an attempt to cover up my intimidation at Kawasaki's sharp eyes and started over. "So basically, all that's different compared with middle school is the ratio of types that make up the student body. And everyone starts acting all high school-ish. That gets annoying."

"Huh? 'Ish'?" Taishi cocked his head as if he couldn't quite parse what I meant.

"I don't know what you're expecting," I said, "but ultimately, most people in high school have this obsession with the 'high schooler' you often seen in fiction, so they put on an act in an attempt to become that. And it just leaves you cold."

I bet that somewhere out there is an unwritten rule. *All high school students must be thus!*

The Law of the High School Student:

Rule the first: Those who would be in high school are obligated to have a girlfriend or boyfriend.

Rule the second: Those who would be in high school must be surrounded by crowds of friends and be obnoxiously rowdy.

Rule the third: Those who would be in high school must act just like the students on TV and in movies.

Any who disobey the above laws are ordered to commit seppuku.

Something like that.

You could say it's similar to how the Shinsengumi—especially that samurai code fundamentalist Toshizou Hijikata—yearned to be like samurai precisely because they were not in fact samurai.

And if you want to reconcile that ideal with reality, eventually, you have no choice but to be unreasonable. For example, a guy who wants girls to like him will check up on how they're doing and annoy them with e-mails, and when he finds a good opportunity, he'll buy them meals and be loud and make a scene in order to draw attention to himself. Even though, in truth, he might be more of a quiet guy. Or maybe a girl wants to be closer to her friends and wears clothes that are in style (LOL), drags herself to group dates so they have the right number of girls, and acts all excited when she listens to the latest J-pop, even though her tastes might be more modest and reserved. Despite it all, these people put in all this effort because they don't want to be cut off from what's "normal." Because they don't want to remove themselves from the value system that "everyone" shares.

Taishi moaned. "That doesn't sound very nice…" As he listened to me, his expression turned dark and gloomy.

"Well, this is just from the perspective of a twisted guy who overthinks everything," I said. "If you want to make friends, you have to be prepared to sacrifice something." Living a life different from others is difficult in its own way, but going with the flow is really hard. Life is hard.

"Whoops! Everyone's glasses are empty, huh?" Komachi said, as if attempting to lighten up the somewhat heavy mood. Humming cheerfully, she gathered up all the cups and glasses, apparently intending to get refills for everyone.

Kawasaki noticed that and immediately stood up. "I'll come with you. That's a lot for one person to carry." Komachi gratefully accepted the offer, and the pair headed off to the drink bar together. For some reason or another, I watched them go.

Then Taishi lifted his head suddenly as if he had just remembered something. He glanced over at the girls' backs where they stood away from us and then leaned toward me, clearing his throat. "Ahem… It's sorta, I dunno, maybe it's weird to ask you about this, but…," Taishi whispered as a preface. "Be honest—what are the girls like there? Are they cute? Like, that Yukinoshita girl is gorgeous, isn't she?"

Oh-ho, so this was the real issue at hand, huh? So he was so worked up at first because he wanted to talk about this. I considered the question for a bit. Yeah, well, if I had to say, I do feel like there are a lot of cute girls at Soubu High.

Or more to the point, the only girls at school whose looks leave an impression on me are the cute ones and the ones you remember like a punch to the face. I don't really remember the normal ones. "There are a lot of cute girls," I said. "There's one class called the International Curriculum, and ninety percent of them are girls. So inevitably, there's more girls than guys, meaning there's a higher than normal ratio of pretty girls."

"Whoa! What a dreamy situation!"

Huh? Sounds like the Bandai corporate slogan. "Dreams and Creation" or something like that, right? Anyway, there was something I had to tell him. "But you know, Taishi…" I expressed it as simply and clearly as I could. "Hasn't your mother told you? You might like a cute girl, but she's not going to like you back."

"I—I understand so much now!" Taishi's high spirits suddenly evaporated, and his eyes opened wide as if he had just been granted divine revelation via lightning strike.

"It's vital to maintain a resigned state of mind," I told him. "If pressing on doesn't work, throw in the towel. Your rule of thumb needs to be 'When the going gets tough, give up.'" These days, I also like to say *Know others and know thyself, and thou shalt retreat from one hundred battles*. "I mean, do you actually think it's possible to get close to a girl like Yukinoshita?"

"You're right… Not for me, at least! She's pretty scary!"

What an open and honest opinion. I'd like to present him with a variety pack of axes.

Yukinoshita is far more unattainable than a flower on a high peak. She's a flower blooming on the Guiana Highlands. Someone who doesn't know much about her might find her rather frightening, seriously overbearing, and highly arrogant. I felt the same way at first…well, um, if you count our encounter in the clubroom as our first meeting, anyway.

Taishi groaned. "Soubu High must be terrifyin' for y'all…"

For some reason, I found Taishi's shivering and faux-Kansai accent rather grating, so I decided to go ahead and keep up the attack. "Your environment might change, but you won't. The whole idea that things will change once you're in high school is an illusion. Stop dreaming." *First, I'll destroy that screwed-up illusion of yours!* Ha-ha, well, I'd briefly had expectations of that nature, too. But such a high school experience is just a faraway ideal. Offering lessons in reality is its own form of kindness.

"Hey, don't bully him so much," Komachi said as she returned, setting down the drinks and poking me in the head.

Noooo, this isn't bullying; I was just teeeeasing him a little, I muttered in my head, the irritating excuse of a little kid. That's exactly what they say, you know.

Kawasaki sat down beside her brother, put her cup to her lips, and said, "Taishi, don't take him too seriously. And more importantly… what you need to be thinking about is getting in."

Taishi flinched once in his chair and groaned.

"Are you expecting to have trouble?" I asked.

Taishi seemed hard-pressed for a reply, so Kawasaki replied instead. "To be honest, right now it's looking a little rough. That's why I'm always telling him to study, but…"

Hanging his head, Taishi slumped and groaned some more.

Komachi came in to encourage him and smooth things over. "It's okay, Taishi! Even if you end up at a different school from me and not Soubu High, I'll still be your friend! I'll be your friend, no matter what!"

"W-we'll be friends no matter what…? O-oh…"

"Yeah, totally friends! Primate, hominid, friend! ♪" She struck the finishing blow.

As her brother, I was okay with that, but as a fellow guy, I almost sympathized with him. His crushed hopes were worthy of *some* pity.

"Well, um, I guess...you need a goal or something?" I suggested. "If you have a clear reason you want to go to that school, you can try harder, right?" I said.

Taishi lifted his head. "A goal?"

"Yeah," I replied. "I can't exactly brag about this, but when I was in middle school, I wanted to go to a school that wouldn't have a single person from my middle school, so I worked my butt off. There's only, like, one person every year that goes from my old middle school to Soubu High."

"You're right—you can't brag about that..." Kawasaki's smile was bitter. I suppose it was the coffee.

"Just so you know," Komachi butted in, "I'm working hard to get in because it's your school, Bro!" The girl took the opportunity to show off.

"Yeah, yeah, I know, I know." I treated her boasting with casual disdain.

Taishi turned back to Kawasaki with a serious expression. "Did you have a reason, too?" he asked.

Kawasaki set down the cup in her hand with a clink. "I... Never mind about me." She had seemed to be thinking about it, but then she swiftly looked away.

I had a vague idea of what her motivation was, though. If she could communicate that to Taishi, maybe it could motivate him, too.

"...Well, our school's a pretty good choice if you're aiming for a public university with low tuition fees," I said.

"You keep your mouth shut!" Panicking, Kawasaki glared at me. But her embarrassed blush didn't have much punch to it.

Fool. A glare from a girl with a brother complex is nothing to fear.

That appeared to be enough for Taishi. He gave a small nod. "Oh..."

I'm sure there are lots of different motivations out there—and not just for Saki Kawasaki. Some people just pick whatever. Some are determined to get one particular school. Not everyone deals with the question in a proactive and focused way. But I think that as long as you make the choice yourself, even if it's based on pessimism or a cowardly process of elimination, it's enough.

"I've made up my mind," said Taishi. "I'm going to Soubu High School!" He looked like a burden had been lifted from his shoulders.

"Well, good luck," I said, completely sincere. …*Wait, Komachi wants to attend my school, doesn't she?* "…If you make it, I'll give you a big hug. Like a sumo wrestler."

"I think he's gonna kill me!" Taishi said, sounding a little scared. His sister moved in to protect him, giving me a rather harsh look.

In an attempt to evade her wrath, I checked the receipt. "Are we done here?" I asked. "Me and Komachi have to get home." According to the clock, it was almost dinnertime. I pulled a thousand-yen bill from my wallet, left it on the table, and stood up.

"Yep!" Taishi rose to his feet and handed me a bill. "Thank you so much, Bro!"

"No, no." I waved his reply away. "The possibility that you'd ever be able to call me 'Bro' completely vanished just a moment ago."

"Wait, that's the part you're saying no to?!" Taishi was shocked.

Komachi watched our exchange out of the corner of her eye, putting her pointer finger on her chin and tilting her head. "Hmm? But if you and Saki get married, Bro, he can call you that, right?"

"D-don't be stupid! Th-that would n-never happen!" I heard someone stuttering behind me as we left the restaurant.

After checking to make sure Kawasaki wouldn't hear, I smirked and muttered, "No kidding. I'd only ever marry a woman willing to support me."

"There it is!" cried Komachi. "Your nasty self-defense mechanisms."

"Hey, cut it out. Don't call it a self-defense mechanism." I mean, it's not a mechanism. Calling it *someone willing to support me* is an absolute defensive front.

All quiet on the defensive front.

Hachiman's mobile

FROM Hachiman 18:07
TITLE Re
Who?

FROM Hachiman 18:10
TITLE Re3
My personal information is all over the place now, huh? What do you want? And who are you?

FROM Hachiman 18:15
TITLE Re5
I haven't done anything to be thanked for, though. And who are you?

FROM Hachiman 18:21
TITLE Re7
In the bath? Oh?

FROM Hachiman 18:22
TITLE Re9
Define the word *clothing* in detail.
Does underwear count as clothes?

FROM Hachiman 18:26
TITLE Re11
U? What's that supposed to mean? Short for *underwear*?
It's too short. I don't get it.

FROM Hachiman 18:44
TITLE Re13
Damn brocon…

Hachiman and Taishi's (and Saki's) mobile chat one day

Taishi's mobile

FROM Taishi 18:05
TITLE None

This is Taishi Kawasaki! Thank you so much for today! You really helped me get motivated!

FROM Taishi 18:08
TITLE Re2

I wrote my name, you know! It's Taishi Kawasaki!

FROM Taishi 18:10
TITLE Re4

I'm e-mailing to say thank you. It's Taishi Kawasaki!

FROM Taishi 18:20
TITLE Re6

My sister said I didn't have to e-mail you, but I'd like to give you a proper thanks. Right now, I have the chance since she's in the bath! I'm Taishi Kawasaki!

FROM Taishi 18:22
TITLE Re8

You're not going to ask me who I am?! I'll be in trouble if my sister comes out without her clothes on.

FROM Taishi 18:24
TITLE Re10

U

FROM Taishi 18:30
TITLE Re12

It's short for "U wanna die"? If you put weird stuff into his head again, I'll kill you.

3

Saika Totsuka has surprisingly subdued tastes.

What exactly counts as a boy? That oft-discussed margin is situated on the line between child and adult in the interval known as puberty. But is the line in middle school? How about high school? Or is it getting a full-time job, or turning twenty? If it's after you get a job, I'll be a boy forever.

Anyway, questions like these have no easy answers, but watching anime sprawled out on the sofa as I am right now, I think it's safe to categorize me as a boy. Still, it's untrue to say that watching anime makes you a kid. There are full-fledged adults out there who have even made a career out of it. That's why everyone needs to buy the DVDs, or they won't be able to make any more. Forget about second seasons—the industry as a whole will shrink, and it'll be harder to make new shows at all. Everyone, please do buy Blu-rays and DVDs.

I'm getting sidetracked.

What I'm trying to say is: I believe it's impossible to differentiate man from boy on the basis of hobbies. So what should form the crux of our definition of *boy*?

There was one particular reason I had come to confront this difficult question. That reason was a single e-mail.

Hello! You free today??

It was only one line, but I'd never seen a text so heartwarming. I wanted to read the Japanese sentence aloud. Heck, I could belt it out in song. It could win an award.

The e-mail I had received from Saika Totsuka the previous night was what had prompted my agonizing over this "boy" problem. What exactly counts as a boy? It was difficult to resolve the issue based on social status, age, or hobby, and furthermore, I had now come to the conclusion that it was even difficult to define a boy on the basis of sex. The laws of the universe mean nothing...

I have not done nearly enough sampling to determine the truth of this matter. Thus, I endeavored to collect further data. I composed a reply that was literally around five hundred characters long, a continuous string of emotes and emojis that I normally never use. Of course, I didn't forget to phrase the end as a question.

As we exchanged e-mails for a while, a certain euphoria overtook me. Anything that gives you so much bliss could legitimately be designated a drug.

And that's how I made a date to hang out with Totsuka. Who cares about issues or conundrums or whatever!

X X X

It was almost time for our rendezvous. When you mess with August, you're playing with fire, and the brilliant sun shone down on me as a lukewarm breeze blew by as strong as life itself. The heat and humidity indexes were about to reach unpleasant levels, as they were apt to during this season. Still, despite the weather, I caught sight of a certain someone who always reminded me of puppies and kittens and the power of love. When my eyes locked on him, he noticed me in the crowd and ran up to me. Cool and swift as the winter wind, emotions whirled in my heart...

Now that I've found Totsuka, that fabulous shimmer, the glow in my heart, I'm ultra-happy! Totsuka is coming!

"Sorry I'm late, Hachiman!" Totsuka, boyishly dressed, leaned over with his hands on his knees after his run and let out a deep exhale.

"Don't worry about it," I said. "I just came a little early." *Only three hours or so. Don't worry about it at all.* "Besides, you're not really late. You didn't have to run."

"Huh? Yeah. But I found you, so." Totsuka laughed, as if to mask his shyness.

My eyes couldn't handle so much pure light at once, and I'm not talking about the sun. Flustered, I looked away. "All right. So what's the plan?"

In our e-mails, all we had agreed on was that we would meet up. We had concluded it would be more fun to decide what to do once we were together, so inevitably, I had spent the whole night evaluating places to go and hadn't gotten enough sleep. What exactly do teenagers mean when they talk about *hanging out*? I don't know the specifics of that behavior. That was why I didn't know what to suggest. But we'd chosen to meet up at Kaihin-Makuhari Station, and it had most things: arcades, karaoke, a movie theater, a park, and a Mini 4WD race track. And shopping was everywhere. We wouldn't lack for any entertainment.

"Hmm..." Totsuka couldn't come up with a reply straight away. He thought for a moment. "I considered a lot of things, but...I don't really know what you like, Hachiman," he said, *hmm*ing some more. He seemed to be sincerely trying to figure out what I like. It's so rare for me to receive such careful consideration from anyone, I found myself staring at him.

I mean, my acquaintances consist of a very self-centered lot. Be it Yuigahama, Zaimokuza, or Komachi—let's not even talk about Yukinoshita—they're all more or less upfront about their own desires. And Miss Hiratsuka...does she think of anything else? You could make a series based on that woman: *The Teacher's Frustrated Desires.*

But anyway, I have no interests. No one will find any interest in me, I assure you. He can deliberate all day, but he's not gonna get easy answers. Even I barely understand a thing about myself. I've seriously just been lying around for most of summer vacation. I sleep until noon. When I do get up, I only go to the bookstore or the library.

And so, in haste, I proposed a compromise that would also function as an apology to Totsuka. "Let's just wander around for now."

"Yeah, okay," he said. "It'd be faster for the two of us to decide together."

I felt slightly uncomfortable when I heard the words *decide together*. In my life thus far, I had been forced to reach most of my decisions alone, so this was new territory. Totsuka was just so nice, it made me want to decide on our children's names together.

Together, we strolled out of the station into the early afternoon. Still, it was really hot, so I figured it would be a good idea to narrow down which of the several nearby malls we would visit and go from there. We had to decide where to start.

Shopping… There's nothing in particular I want to buy, so scratch that. Arcades… Well, that could work. I doubt Totsuka is into capsule machines, but maybe he'd be into medal games or crane games, so…over this way, I guess…?

I decided to head toward Cineplex Makuhari, a mall that had an arcade I was familiar with. Cineplex may sound like Aniplex, but it belongs to the Kadokawa Group.

Inside was a movie theater with ten screens, an arcade, and a variety of restaurants. When we entered, we were met with a jumble of gaudy decorative lights and pop audio. They didn't have any plain old video games. The theme of the arcade was rhythm and dance games, arcade shooters, medal games, and crane machines, along with photo booths and darts and stuff, too. I guess you'd call it an arcade for active young people. This area was home to a number of high schools and universities, so you could be sure that was their main target market. There were also adjoining restaurants and a movie theater, which suggested they were also counting on demand from the family bracket. We did one full circle around the premises, and then Totsuka suddenly froze.

"What is it?" I asked, eyes following his gaze. He was examining a poster of a movie that was currently playing.

"So it's already out..." He *hmm*ed and kept staring with great interest.

"You wanna watch a movie, then?"

"Oh! We can do something you like!" Totsuka waved his hands, flustered.

"No, let's see a movie. Now that I think about it, this is the first time I've ever seen one with someone other than family. It'll be nice to do it for once." The last time I saw a movie together with another person was when I was really little, at the old Marinpia movie theater that isn't there anymore. We were basically imprisoned while my mom was shopping, though.

Ever since middle school, I've been going alone. There's a movie theater close to my house, so it's the perfect place to just wander into when I'm out and about.

Totsuka contemplated for a bit and then hesitantly locked eyes with me. "Can we?"

When he asked like that, I could only give him one answer. "Yeah."

I've decided! Totsuka will be my first!

X X X

Surprisingly enough, Totsuka picked a horror movie. We chose our seats and bought our tickets at the counter. Adjacent seats in the back—25E and 25F.

It was summer vacation, but that really only applied to students. For adults with regular jobs, it was just another weekday, so the theater wasn't too crowded. That also meant that most of the customers at this time were students. In fact, all the stupid, obnoxious couples were having a ball screeching to each other about how lucky they were the theater was empty.

I thought I saw someone who could be Miura among the squawking mass of trash, but I figured it was just my imagination. *Why do those types all look and dress the same? I can't tell them apart. Are they clones? No one is less unique than people who go on about uniqueness. The more you know.*

And then you have the ones who confuse wearing a trench coat in the middle of summer for individuality. The guy sitting in the front row panting like a grizzly was a good example. My instincts were sounding the alarm, warning me not to look, so I obeyed and chose instead to look for our seats. In the characteristic silence and faint tension that occurs before a movie, I walked up the aisle, scanning the seat numbers on each row. Totsuka, who had taken the lead at the entrance, found our seats, waving me over with tiny motions of his hand. I guess he was trying to be considerate and keep quiet in the theater.

I leaned back deeply into my seat and dropped my forearm onto the armrest. I had assumed the stately, calm, and self-possessed posture of a demon king.

Then a soft, light sensation brushed against my hand on the armrest.

"Oh, sorry." When Totsuka apologized, I realized what had touched me. It had been Totsuka's hand.

I've touched an angel! "N-no! I'm sorry!" I said, and both of us jerked our hands away at the same time.

"..."

"..."

We looked away as an oddly awkward silence fell over us. I sneaked a peek at Totsuka from the corner of my eye to see his shoulders hunched. He was looking down in apparent embarrassment.

**However, we are both guys.*

In the air-conditioned theater, my arm itched where that faint warmth had touched me.

**However, we are both guys.*

We exchanged glances, as if searching for the right moment to speak. "Y-you can use it, Hachiman," Totsuka whispered quietly.

"No, I'm right-handed, so I put more weight on the right side! I'm totally fine! The left hand is just for support!" For some reason, that was my flustered excuse.

Totsuka giggled. "You're so funny," he said. "Then let's share. Half and half." He daintily laid his elbow on about one-third of the available space.

"O-okay…" Timidly, nervously, I laid my left hand on the armrest as well.

Ohh, my left hand… My left hand is so happy! *Hooray for world peace!*

If the world consisted of one hundred Totsukas, I'm sure there would be no war. Weapons dealers and their ilk would go out of business. Everything stressful would disappear. He's like lavender. The ever-obnoxious movie thief's wiggly anti-piracy dance didn't get on my nerves that day.

X X X

The movie was approaching its climax.

I think. I'm not really sure…

I didn't even know how much time had passed, never mind what was going on on-screen. It felt like an hour, even two, or maybe it was only ten minutes. Time flies when you're having fun. By my internal clock, it wouldn't even be an hour. An observer's perception of time is subjective.

"Ahh!"

Totsuka yelped, clinging to my shirt with his tiny shoulders trembling as a ghost in a white dress emerged from the screen in 3D.

Oh, that startled me. Man, even I felt like my heart might stop just now. He was just so adorable…

Scared Totsuka is cute. Totsucute.

After that, the ghost in the white dress crawled out of the screen again and again. Each and every time, Totsuka would gulp and let out tiny *eeps*.

Man, this movie really is scary. I'm beyond just stepping off the right path; at this rate, I'm about to clear the entire Totsuka route. Terrifying. If he gets scared enough to wrap his arms around me, I'll be cringing into my seat in terror. Actually, I'd probably need to lean forward.

My heart groaned under the strain, and my blood raged like a torrent of muddy water. They've got to prepare the ATM just in case it gives out. Or wait, or was that thing called an ETC? EVA? Whatever. It looks like it's going to be over soon. Summoning all my willpower not to think about Totsuka's presence, I decided to casually glance around the theater. What I really wanted to do was calm myself down by listing prime numbers, but sadly, as a humanities type, I couldn't figure out if zero counted or not and immediately gave up.

The air-conditioned theater was chilly. Combined with the darkness, it was the optimum environment for watching a horror movie.

By the time the end credits rolled, I still had no idea what happened in the film. Totsuka patiently waited until all the lines of text finished scrolling, and then we stood almost simultaneously. Basking in the afterglow, I walked out of the theater with a leisurely stride.

"That was so much fun!" exclaimed Totsuka. "But I was screaming the whole time, so my throat's a little dry."

"Yeah, I'm thirsty, too." All that weird anxiety had not only made me thirsty, it had made my shoulders stiff.

We joined the flow of people leaving the theater and continued out the exit, down to where it connected to an outdoor staircase. Having finally begun its decent, the sun was blocked from view by a tower, and a breeze blew across the shadow that gently lay over us.

"You wanna go sit down for a while over there?" I pointed at a café nearby at the bottom of the stairs, and Totsuka nodded. A few of our fellow moviegoers were here and there, but there were still seats available for two people. We walked straight in and quickly ordered at the register.

"Um, iced coffee," I said.

"Oh, I'll have one, too, then," said Totsuka.

"Herm. Then I, too, shall indulge in a chilled coffee."

All three of us ordered iced coffee, so there was no wait. We got our drinks and headed over to occupy a nearby table.

First, I drank a few sips while it was still black, enjoying the essential flavor of the coffee. The crisp bitterness woke up my eyes. Then I added some creamer and liquid sugar. I call this stage Black RX. Yep, I liked it sweet! After moistening our throats, all three of us breathed short, relaxed sighs.

All three of us?

"...Hold on a minute," I said.

"Huh?" said Totsuka.

"Herm?"

Don't give me that. I'm talking about you.

The suspicious, bearlike, trench coat–clad individual was sitting with us like he had every right to be there. Yeah, I'd had the feeling he was around. "Um, who are you again?" I asked. "Was it Shinkiba?"

"It's Zaimokuza, Hachiman." *Totsuka actually gave me a serious reply...*

"Well, I don't care if he's a Zaimoku or a Kimuraya or what. Where did you crawl out from? Are you one of those bugs that are everywhere? Are you a maize weevil or something?" Or perhaps a varied carpet beetle?

Zaimokuza slurped hard from his straw and raised his head. "Herm. I glimpsed you at the movie theater, and I considered calling out to you, but then I started tracking you and just ended up coming here. Mm-hmm, it seems my active camouflage is in good shape today, as usual."

"I think everyone was just pretending not to see you," I said. Well, the reason I hadn't noticed was because I had eyes only for Totsuka, though.

"I haven't seen you in a while, Zaimokuza," Totsuka said to him.

"I-indeed. Mwa-ha-ha-ha-ha!" Zaimokuza cackled rather anxiously.

Actually, Totsuka's ability to automatically accept him is downright remarkable. Well, he's capable of talking with me, so I guess it's no wonder he can talk to Zaimokuza, too.

"So you saw the same movie?" I asked.

"That I did," he replied. "But this one was a dud. The unique malice of Japanese horror was missing. 'Twas most pathetic garbage. Fweh-heh! Though 'twas but a horror movie, I am rather an eccentric. When I enjoy a film, I see it not as what is oft called a 'Hollywood-ized' form of mass entertainment but rather as a work of art. I suppose 'tis the influence of Lafcadio Hearn. *Ah-hur-hurr!* Whoops, I guess I let you see my in-depth knowledge there. No disrespect, oh no, *fluherple*! While this may appear to suggest I am an *otaku*, I am most certainly not an *otaku*. Lulz!!"

There he goes... M-2 syndrome types like him are unusually knowledgeable regarding the occult, which can be awkward. They have a half-baked understanding of literary types like Yakumo Koizumi and Kyouka Izumi and also some figures in the study of folk custom, like Kunio Yanagita and Shinobu Orikuchi, but they also have the unfortunate habit of compulsively flaunting their knowledge in detail.

I had ignored the last half of Zaimokuza's rambling, but Totsuka had listened intently until the very end. He's so kind, I bet he could get away with charging for it. "You think? I like those kind of movies a lot, though," said Totsuka.

"Indeed. As do I," replied Zaimokuza.

"Huh?!"

Zaimokuza's U-turn was quick and slick. He'd changed his mind so quickly, I could almost see the flash. "Wow," I commented. "You flip-flopped like a politician."

"You be silent!" he said. "What did you think of the film, Hachiman?"

"It was all spectacle and easy to follow. Doesn't matter how good it was." I mean, I had been watching Totsuka for the whole film, but I'd still gotten a vague idea of the premise.

"Yeah!" agreed Totsuka. "The things coming out of the screen right in your face were spectacular. They got me every time! I thought my heart would stop!"

I feel like my heart is going to stop right this minute. Before Totsuka and his wild gestures, enthusiastically reenacting those scenes, my heart might wear itself out.

"Well, 'twas no botheration for me, since I no longer experience fear," said Zaimokuza as he began trembling like a leaf. "She Who Must Not Be Named is far more fearsome...*foy*." He was indeed like Malfoy, quivering in terror before the memory of Lord Voldemort. The only person I could imagine inspiring that much dread in him was Yukinoshita.

"Yeah, true. Yukinoshita is scarier," I said.

"Hachiman, that's a mean thing to say," said Totsuka. "It's true that...at first...um...she did scare me a little...but..." His indignant reprimand gradually deflated. "She acts dignified and serious, so she might come off as scary," he finished.

"She's also so honest, it's terrifying," I said.

"You never know what she's going to say to you," Zaimokuza added.

Well, when you go to watch a movie or something with another person, you're not going to experience it the same way as they would. You might hold similar impressions, but the similarity is proof that something is definitely different. Everyone sees only what they want to see. There are as many interpretations as there are individuals—be they of movies or of people.

That's why it's presumptuous to believe you can really understand something. Acting like you do is a sin; it is evil. But even so, you have no choice but to live your life pretending you do. In life, you must both understand and be understood, while both you and those around you minutely redefine what is you and what is them based on vague knowledge that both you and they will disseminate to everyone else. If you don't do that, your identity will vanish like so much mist. That's just how vague and uncertain identity is. The more you think about it, the less you understand it, like *Gestaltzerfall.* Every time your images crumble, you pick up what little scraps of remaining information you have and reconstruct your image of you and them. But they are merely primitive and crude images you'll interpret however you can, like the simulacrum phenomenon.

If you want to talk horror, that's horror.

I suddenly felt a chill in the air-conditioned café. Hunching my shoulders, I willed myself not to shiver. I picked up my glass and noticed it was empty. As I gave up and put it down, Zaimokuza continued the conversation.

"But 'twas a good breather. Now I can go back to concentrating on my book. Oh yeah, Hachiman, d-do you want to…look at my draft?"

Don't give me that blushy little glance. It's not cute. "If it's actually done," I replied. "Wait—do you have it with you right now?"

"Herm, of course," he said. "He who would be a writer is ready to compose anywhere, at any time. I perpetually have my writing devices close at hand—my laptop, Pomera, tablet, and smartphone." He looked so proud.

Yeah, some guys are like that… They think just collecting all the tools is enough to have done the task.

Totsuka faced Zaimokuza, respect in his eyes. "Then you're always working hard on your book, huh?"

"Oh, I don't know about that," I said. I can confidently assure you Zaimokuza is not working hard at all. The more someone plays the writer and expounds upon creativity, the fewer words they've actually put on a page. I needed to hammer this in, both to caution Totsuka and to prevent him from cultivating a weird sense of admiration for Zaimokuza. Maybe I should hammer some nails into Zaimokuza's head, too.

Zaimokuza seemed to pick up on my disdain, as he was visibly offended. "Ha-fumf! How insolent. I do not want to hear that from you. Are you aught but idle?"

"Hmm. I guess not. I'm just going to summer classes. Then I did that independent research project."

"Huh? Was that part of our homework?" Totsuka panicked. From his expression, he had been relaxing in the knowledge that he'd already finished his summer homework.

"No, my sister's," I replied.

"Oh, Komachi's project, huh?" he said. "You're a good brother, Hachiman."

"Not really. If I were really a good brother, I would have made her do it herself."

"What was the topic of this project?" Zaimokuza asked.

"I just threw together random stuff I found on the Internet."

"Huh?" asked Totsuka. "Are you allowed to do that?"

"Herm," said Zaimokuza. "Well, 'tis meant to be an independent effort, so I doubt a trifle like that would bother them. In fact, if you get too serious about the project, everyone else will think you're weird."

"Yep," I agreed. "Especially because Komachi is a girl. I hear it's best not to get too into this kind of thing." The only thing Komachi had requested about the project is that I should keep it unexceptional and down-to-earth. Come on, that's a cruel request for a guy like me—if I have to, I'll fly higher than Dhalsim. I'll launch myself so high above the stratosphere of what is acceptable, you might as well call me her space brother.

But now that he mentioned it, I do remember one time I put all this effort into an independent research project and then everyone giggled at me for it. I really wish the teacher hadn't displayed it over the cabinets at the back of the classroom.

"Those are always so hard, huh? You can never think of anything original to do," Totsuka said, sounding a little nostalgic.

When you're told you can pick anything, rarely can you actually think of something. I'm not Inventor Boy Kanipan. "That's the real test of your IQ," I said. "In my opinion, there's meaning in testing your creativity and stuff, not just your ability to cram in facts."

"You seem like you'd be good at that, Zaimokuza," said Totsuka. "I mean, since you're aiming to be a writer."

"He doesn't seem like he has a very high IQ, though," I said.

"Herm, well," said Zaimokuza, "I have a high EQ. My sensitivity is very robust."

EQ—that is to say, emotional intelligence. This is just my personal opinion, but I think everyone who brings up EQ when you're talking about IQ, without exception, has low IQ. If they bring up E.T., they're Spielberg. And just so you know, if they bring up ED, then they're Pelé.

"Oh yeah," I added. "And there was that guy who brought his Mini 4WD and said he made it himself." The moment I said that, Zaimokuza's whole body twitched, and he started sweating for some reason. *Is this guy a toad or something?*

"H-huh? Um, H-H-H-Hachiman, did you go to my elementary school?"

"So, you were one of *those* kids, huh? And don't get out of character over a little remark like that." Actually, I just want him to get out, period.

"I used to have a Mini 4WD," said Totsuka.

"That's surprising...," I commented.

"Huh? Why? I'm a boy, too." He giggled.

I tried to imagine Totsuka as a boy playing with a Mini 4WD, but for some reason an image of him wearing a baseball hat, T-shirt, and leggings popped into my mind. I bet he was cute. Whoops, correction: He's still cute. They should write that he was cute in times past in *Konjaku Monogatari* and teach it in schools.

"Ha-mumph. But none could match my Brocken G," said Zaimokuza. "I had it outfitted with a real hammer. In a head-on collision, it would destroy any opponent without exception."

"That is the stupidest thing you could do... Ugh, I put a box-cutter blade on my Beak Spider, though, so I can't talk..." I also attached the marking pin from a sewing set onto my Ray Stinger.

"That stuff's dangerous, you know," Totsuka scolded us.

Zaimokuza and I looked at each other. "Relax," I said. "I just played with it all by myself."

"Indeed. Loners hurt no one. They hurt only themselves."

"You're not allowed to hurt yourself!"

"Okay…" With Totsuka glaring at me, I was sincerely sorry.

"H-herm… B-but I can do legitimate tune-ups, too!" Zaimokuza said. "I am swift like the wind in every race!"

I was getting sick of his declarations. "…What? You think you can beat me? *Me*, and my Beak Spider? With its small one-way wheels, reston sponge tires, and torque-tuned high-speed gears inside a slim and lightweight body for added air cooling; a stabilizer ball for handling high-speed turns; and a converted aluminum downthrust roller? It's theoretically as fast as you can get!" I had always played with it alone, so I'd never tested it out. I mean, my parents never bought me a course for it. I used to make my own with cardboard and stuff, but the car just got caught on the tape and didn't work very well.

Zaimokuza smiled boldly and chuckled. "Heh-heh-heh. Converted aluminum? What utter ignorance… That heavy weight will spell your doom."

"Yeah, right. My Beak Spider's low center of gravity makes it stable. That's where the power comes from."

"Oh-ho…then shall we settle this with a duel?"

Zaimokuza and I faced each other, glaring as hard as we could. I was inches from punching the air in front of me and yelling out *Go! Maaaaagnum!* Wait, that's Galactica Magnum.

We wordlessly exchanged scowls until the silence between us was broken by a rather unexpected statement.

"Oh, that's so nice!" exclaimed Totsuka. "It's been so long since I last raced. I'd love to do it again! My Avante was pretty fast."

""Avante?!""

Why is his from a different generation?! What refined taste, too! So he's not a mainstream Boomerang or Emperor sort of guy, huh?

…But, well, I guess I shouldn't be too surprised that we're of different generations. It's been years since I last played with my Mini 4WD, but the passion of that era still lives within me. I still pretend my umbrella's a sword after it rains, saving the world over and over in my imaginary world. I'll probably still remember it, even as an adult. No matter your generation, ultimately, at the root, you don't change. That's why my time as a boy will never end.

Hachiman and Zaimokuza's mobile chat one day

Zaimokuza's mobile

FROM Zaimokuza 23:32
TITLE None

Herm. Is it OK if I attach my draft in an e-mail?

FROM MAILER-DAEMON 23:32
TITLE Returned mail: see transcript for details

This message was undeliverable due to the following reason…

FROM Zaimokuza
TITLE None

You have changed your e-mail, you say?! Hachiman! Hachimaaaaaaan!

FROM MAILER-DAEMON
TITLE Returned mail: see transcript f

This message was undeliverable due to the following reason…

4

Unfortunately, nobody knows where **Shizuka Hiratsuka**'s red thread went.

What is the greatest food of all? Is it curry? Shabu-shabu? Sushi? Soba? Sukiyaki, BBQ, or sweets?

It is none of these. Ramen is the greatest. *Ramen.*

For a solitary high school boy, it's one of the nearest and dearest. When you're pondering what to eat, ramen is the first thing that comes to mind. You can stop by your usual haunt on the way back from school. You can discover a new place while you're out shopping and wander on in. If you get hungry in the middle of the night, you can boil some water and slurp that cup ramen down.

But to all you couples who go to a ramen shop for a date…

…you guys suck.

Don't take forever blathering to each other at the counter. People are lining up to get in. Do all your mushy stuff at the Starbucks, since you guys love that place so much. Don't share how in love you are at the ramen shop counter. Consider all the people you're forcing to watch as they wait in line right behind you.

Ramen is, at its core, a solitary meal. If you chat, the broth gets cold and the noodles get soggy. That's why Ichiran's "flavor concentration system" is the great invention of the ramen world. They have divisions between every seat at the counter, and they even hang up curtains in front of the kitchen so they can't see the customers from in there. They used to have *patent pending* written on those division things... I wonder if they got that patent.

I'm getting sidetracked.

Basically, ramen is the food most appropriate for someone of my stature. It is a supreme dish that heals the noble souls of those who persist in the principles of isolation.

That is ramen.

X X X

As often happens in summer, I woke up at an awkward time and missed a meal. Some may be of the opinion that, at times like these, one who aspires to be a stay-at-home husband should make something to eat himself. But that is sheer naïveté. A *real* stay-at-home wife hands her husband a five-hundred-yen coin for his lunch and then treats herself to an extravagant lunch with his money. You might call this view narrow-minded, but that's the kind of househusband I want to be. Also, when we divorce, I want a huge settlement.

So, since I aspire to be a stay-at-home husband, I played out the ideal and headed out for an extravagant lunch. I've recently received a windfall, thanks to my alchemy scheme of pocketing the scholarship money from prep school. I'm a full-wallet alchemist. And for lunch that day, I settled on ramen. Once I've made the decision, my stomach will hardly accept anything else.

Chiba is a competitive market for ramen. Matsudo, Chiba city, Tsudanuma, and Motoyawata—every station has its hotspots. And lately, the fancier types like Takeoka-style and Katsuura-style *tantanmen* have gone national. Well-known shops are an exceptionally safe choice, but once you get used to their food, you really do start wanting to find new places yourself.

When you go out to eat with another person, you compromise and go for what they like. It also makes you want to show off. *I know a pretty good place, you know; isn't that amazing? Heh-heh-heh.* You can't make a proper adventure of it. But when you're alone, you're not concerned with obligations—you can just march into a shop. This proactivity leads you to new discoveries and helps you develop as a foodie. What I'm saying is, a loner is ever overflowing with that pioneering spirit. We are modern adventurers full of the vigorous desire to take a challenge.

That is why, that day, I decided to go to a ramen shop in my own neighborhood, where I had not yet done much trailblazing. It's always darkest under the lighthouse, as they say, so braving my personal blind spots in the local area was a fantastic strategy. It was an intellectual move, overturning the logic that prevents Tokyo residents from visiting Tokyo Tower.

After a long, jerky bus ride, I arrived near my destination at Kaihin-Makuhari and set forth. My stride was full of determination.

I would wander around this area on my way home from school, so I'd had my eye on a certain shop for a while now with the intent of giving it a try eventually.

Roasting in the rays of the summer sun, I steadily walked along. The humidity and heat were grating on my nerves, but then a clear sound rang through the area to dispel my irritation. It was the sonorous *ding-dong, ding-dong* of a church bell.

The area was lined with tall hotels and a large number of wedding venues. The church was one such venue, so it was probably hosting a wedding now. Merriment filled the air, and even out in the street, I could hear voices beyond the fence shouting their congratulations. It was the first time I'd ever seen something like this, so I took a little peek. What I saw was a joyous scene like something out of a photograph.

But wait, what was that? Out of the corner of my eye, I noticed something like a black stain… I rubbed my eyes vigorously and gave the area a hard look. I was not preoccupied with a single spot. I saw everything in its entirety…effortlessly. That is what it means to truly "see," or so I hear. Following the teachings of Oshou Takuan, I gazed intently at the black shadow. Whoever it was, was swathed in garments of black, the sole source of negative energy. The darkness was absorbing all the light around it, bending even the rays of the sun. It was the one spot of wrongness, clinging to that happy display like a grudge and quietly muttering, "Drop dead, amen…"

Oh… I definitely know that person…

"I hope you get married soon, too."

"It'll be your turn next, Shizu!"

"Shizu, Aunt, I found another good one! I think it'll go well this time. Why don't you try meeting him, Shizu?"

"I've started saving for grandchildren, Shizu."

With each comment, the black stain twitched and swayed. The spiritual pressure…disappeared…?

I think I just saw something I shouldn't have. I quickly averted my eyes, pretending to be none the wiser, and began walking away. But you must never forget…When you gaze into the void, the void will gaze back at you…

All of a sudden, the one I was watching yelled, "H-Hikigaya!"

The nearby middle-aged couples peered in my direction. I found myself bowing, and they bowed back. *What the heck are we doing? Does this count as meeting the parents? Do I have no choice now but to take responsibility, marry her, and have her support me?*

The dark blemish on the proceedings turned to the couples and rapidly explained, "Th-that over there is one of my problem kids! Th-this is work! J-just so you know!" Heels clicking on the sidewalk, the shadow ran toward me. "Hikigaya! Perfect timing! What a relief!" said the black stain—who was actually a pretty lady in a black dress, now that I saw her up close—as she grasped my hand, gleefully vacating the premises.

"Huh? Hey, um…" When a pretty older woman grabs your hand, can you do anything besides obediently following along? We walked for a while until we rounded a corner, entered a park, and stopped.

The lady breathed a visible sigh of relief. "I managed to get away for now." Her black party dress hugged the smooth curves and contours of her body, and a fur collar brilliantly decorated the white nape of her neck. Her hair, in an updo, was a glamorous pitch-black that could have been made for that dress. Her hand, grasping mine through black gloves that matched the dress, was surprisingly soft.

"Um...," I said.

"Hmm? Oh, sorry to do this out of the blue." The posh beauty gave me a broad smile and drew me to a bench, taking out a cigarette and tapping it to pack the tobacco inside. It was jarring, considering her appearance. Like something an old man would do. The cigarette sizzled as she ignited it with a hundred-yen lighter. Smoke slowly trailed upward from the tip.

I'd been really confused before since she looked so different from usual, but seeing her in this state, there was no mistaking Shizuka Hiratsuka, the teacher advisor for the Service Club.

Whoa. When she gets all dressed up, she's really pretty. "Um, was it okay for you to slip out?" I asked. "That was a wedding, right?"

"I don't care," she replied. "I already gave my gift."

"But won't there be an after-party and stuff?"

"What's gotten into you? You're being surprisingly considerate."

"No, I mean, it's an important event for meeting men—"

Miss Hiratsuka snorted. "It's my cousin's wedding, so it's not like I'm a guest." She averted her eyes sadly and, with her cigarette still in her mouth, muttered, "I didn't really want to go in the first place. My cousin is younger than me, so I knew he'd be walking on eggshells and my aunts would be constantly making a fuss about getting married. My parents won't shut up about it, either... Seriously, paying money to go to a wedding just to have your family rag on you isn't worth it..." She blew out smoke with a long, long sigh and crushed the cigarette in her hand.

I don't really have anything to say to that...

An odd moment passed before she spoke again, as if she was attempting to pull herself together. "What were you doing around here?"

"I was thinking I'd go have some ramen."

"Ramen! Do people do that?" Suddenly, Miss Hiratsuka was sounding enthusiastic, and her dead eyes sparked with life. "Now that I think of it, after I checked in and everything, I totally didn't get a chance to eat… Perfect. I'll go with you."

"Well, if you want, I guess. It's this way," I said, taking the lead at a steady pace. Miss Hiratsuka followed, heels tapping. *C'mon, she's dressed way too fancy for this! Everyone's looking!*

We came out at a fairly crowded street and encountered a storm of furtive glances from our fellow pedestrians. Miss Hiratsuka's clothing was so fancy, and I mean, she was pretty, so I guess people just couldn't help it. The woman in question didn't seem to care, though, and talked to me the same way she always did. "I've heard you were advising a future Soubu High student," she said. "I'm impressed to hear you've been continuing your Service Club activities during the break. Quite impressed indeed."

"That's not really what happened. And how did you know?" She does the scariest stuff with zero hesitation…

"Your sister told me."

"Since when are you two best friends?" Komachi has encircled me with a net composed of every single one of my acquaintances. It's staggering. Does she have a full ABCD encirclement going on here? Am I gonna be okay? A: Asinine Yuigahama. B: Bonk-to-the-Head Hiratsuka. C: Cute Komachi. D: …Damn, what was her name again? Something-nokawa? In absence of a trade bloc, I must resist them with a mental block.

"She's a good sister," said Miss Hiratsuka. "I almost wish I had a little sister like that. Oh, and I'm not trying to imply anything by saying that, of course."

"Considering the age gap between you and Komachi, she could be your daughter," I cackled.

"Hikigaya…"

Oh, crap. She's gonna punch me! I reflexively closed my eyes shut and braced myself. But the expected fist never came. Curious, I opened my eyes to see a very dejected Miss Hiratsuka.

"Those jokes are a little too much right now."

"I-I'm sorry!" *Hurry! Hurry, someone! Marry this woman! If someone doesn't do it fast, I'll end up marrying her myself. Someone do something. Please.*

X X X

August was coming to a close, but it was still too hot to be out and about. The rays of the sun streaming down gradually heated my skin. But the area was facing the coastal road, and the breeze blowing through offered some relief. Even lining up outside the ramen shop wasn't too uncomfortable.

It would probably take a little longer before we could get into the shop, but I had no trouble, since I'm good at wasting time. I'm also good at wasting other peoples' reputations and laying waste to bubble wrap. These facts would probably lead you to predict I would also be good at wasting office noobs once I'm employed, but noobs are cute, so no way am I getting a job.

I started people-watching. Like the guy in front of us who had been chatting at high volume like his life depended on it for a while, or the two guys behind us who looked like university students and reminded me of a guy and a girl on a date. When I got bored of that, I started fantasizing about what would happen if I opened up a ramen shop and it got popular and I ended up on TV, and how I would respond. First of all, when I drained the noodles, I would whirl them around, call the move *Tsubame Gaeshi*, and then tell everyone it was a family trade secret. When my shop got even more popular, I'd open up a ramen academy and extort money out of white-collar workers dreaming of leaving the rat race. As I was busy zoning out and weaving my ridiculous fantasy, I heard a soft sigh that could have been a chuckle.

"What?" I asked.

When I directed my attention to the source of the sound, Miss Hiratsuka spoke with a wry smile. "Oh, I'm just surprised. I thought for sure you'd hate crowds and lines."

"I do hate them. Chaotic crowds, anyway. Lines, though, they've got a proper system. Some idiots out there like to cut in, though."

I actually don't really mind lines. I think the reason most people hate them is because they feel they're wasting time. When you consider all the urban legends about couples who break up during dates at Destiny Land, you can only presume that frustration with the lines and the ensuing difference in values must have surfaced and driven them to it. But I always have a ludicrous amount of time on my hands, and my abundantly overflowing power of imagination staves off any boredom. Besides, typically, I'm on my own. A steel heart like mine does not waver in the face of a mere queue. But disorderly mobs? They're full of people who can't follow the rules and have no manners. I can't stand looking at them or having them come near me. I just can't.

"You're more fastidious than I imagined," Miss Hiratsuka commented with surprise.

"Not really. I'm not good at cleaning up and stuff." My room is actually pretty dirty. If you labeled it *Urbanization* or *The Future of the World* and displayed it at an art gallery, it would be highly valued after my death.

"I'm not talking about cleanliness or hygiene," she said. "I'm talking about your ideals. Though ultimately, they all revolve around you."

"That's just a technical way of saying I'm a selfish, egocentric bastard."

"It *is* a compliment. Cultivating a proper internal standard of judgment is a good thing."

The amiable gaze she leveled at me was uncomfortable. That hadn't been my intent at all, of course. I turned away from her, quietly muttering, "I just hate rowdy people."

When they're all like, *Ohh, this is sooo much fun* or *This is the best time of our lives!* or whatever, who exactly are they trying to convince? To the introvert, who knows how to enjoy himself quietly through reading or gaming at home, their emphasis on fun, fun, fun sounds groundless, in a way. I disagree that the volume of your voice and the number of people in a gathering is a good metric for fun, and I hate people who are deluded into thinking it is. Maybe they see crowds and events as the ideal time to emphasize that belief, since that's when they're at their worst. I can't stand to watch how fake and phony it all is. How come you can't prove you're having fun—prove that you're right—all by yourself?

If they're going to take pride in that attitude, they need that validation because they lack conviction. Somewhere, their rational selves are asking, *Is this really fun?* And in an attempt to erase that doubt, they deny it verbally. *This is so much fun! What a party! This is awesome! So epic!* They say it out loud. They raise their voices and yell it.

I don't want to be a part of that crowd. I don't want to turn into a phony hypocrite.

"I guess you won't be able to go to the fireworks show, then," said Miss Hiratsuka, cutting my train of thought short.

"Fireworks?"

"Yeah. You know the one I mean, right? At the Port Tower. You're not going?" she asked.

I remembered, now that she mentioned it. The Port Tower fireworks display was a big event synonymous with summer. I've gone before when I was a kid. I don't think I cared much about the fireworks. I'd totally been in it for the food stalls. They don't feel that important when you live around here, since there's fireworks at the stadium when they do night games, and Destiny Land has fireworks all year long. "I don't have any particular plans to go. Are you going, though?" I asked her in return.

She breathed a long sigh. "It's part of the job during summer vacation. It's more like I'm going there to watch people, not fireworks."

Wondering what she was talking about, I silently prompted her to explain.

"I'm being sent out to keep an eye on the students," she said. "I do it for festivals, too. They always make the young teachers handle that sort of legwork. Well, they got me there! Ha-ha-ha-ha! You know, because I'm a young teacher."

"Someone sure sounds happy," I muttered, but I guess she didn't hear.

Seemingly in a good mood, Miss Hiratsuka continued. "We

can't have any of our students getting out of control. It's a municipal event, so a lot of bigwigs attend."

"Oh? Bigwigs?"

"Yes. Yukinoshita's family will probably be there."

Yeah, I suppose you could call the Yukinoshita family regional celebrities, what with her dad being in the prefectural assembly and having a local business. Maybe they're even backing the event in some way or another. It would be natural to invite them, in that case.

"Speaking of which," I said, "was Haruno your student?"

"Hmm? Oh yeah. You guys entered just as she left, huh? She's a Soubu High School alum. I'm impressed you remembered."

If she had left just as we entered, that meant she was three years older, which would make her nineteen or twenty. So she graduated two years ago, huh…?

"Her grades were top-notch, generally speaking, and she excelled at everything she tried. And with those looks, most of the boys treated her like a goddess."

That sure reminded me of a certain someone. Well, that one is more like a witch than a goddess, though. A goddess and a witch… While they were fundamentally the same thing, you'd see one as good and the other as evil depending on your religious view, I bet. The idea fit my image of them perfectly.

"But…" Miss Hiratsuka trailed off, pausing for a moment. With a bitter expression, she continued, "She was not a model student."

"She got good grades, didn't she?"

"She did. But it was only her grades that were good. She was loud in class, she would hike up her skirt and unbutton the top of her blouse, and I'd always see her at fireworks shows and festivals, like I just mentioned. She was always running from place to place looking for fun. Which means she had lots of friends."

Yeah, I could easily imagine her being like that. She was cheerful and willful, and her free nature would most certainly draw people to her.

"But even that was…" Miss Hiratsuka failed to continue, so I finished her sentence.

"You mean that was a mask, too?"

"Oh, so you noticed." Miss Hiratsuka was impressed. Or rather, she was smirking like she was sharing a naughty secret.

"You can tell just by looking at her."

"You're quite insightful."

I guess. It's the boon of my dad's special training for nurturing useless bastards.

"That facade is part of her appeal, though. People who figure out that it's a mask start to like her schemes and stubbornness."

"So she's got charisma," I said.

Miss Hiratsuka nodded. "When she was on the committee for the cultural festival, we had the most participants in school history. She didn't just get students involved; the teachers got in on it, too. They dragged me out and made me play the bass." She grimaced as if the memory was unpleasant. *Huh, I guess she does have a similar hairstyle as that other bass player. I thought we were talking about something-On for a moment there…*

"For sisters, those two really are different, though," I said. If Yukino Yukinoshita was like a graduate student who threw herself into her studies, Haruno Yukinoshita was like some university-going thought leader (LOL). Just so you know, I really hate terms like *thought leader* and *lifespiration* and *networking guru*. Normies (LOL) love words like these. Don't use such strong words. They just make you look weak.

"Yeah." Miss Hiratsuka nodded, but then she folded her arms in thought. "But I'm not saying she should be like Haruno. She just needs to develop her own fortes."

"Fortes?"

"I said it before, didn't I? That's she's kind and generally in the right."

Miss Hiratsuka had indeed appraised her as such in the past. I think she had also said that it would make her life difficult because the world is unkind and full of wrongs. And Yukinoshita is indeed right in most cases. I'm still a little skeptical about the kindness part, but, well, just because someone isn't gentle doesn't mean they're unkind.

I don't need kindness, though. I'd rather be coddled. Maybe strictness is its own form of kindness, but I don't want any of that, no thank you. *I guess Miss Hiratsuka is the tough-love type, too, huh?* I thought, glancing at her.

She was watching me with a warm expression. "You're the same." She flashed a smile at me, but I couldn't figure out what she meant.

"The same as what?"

"You're also kind and accurate with your judgments. Those qualities in you tend to clash with hers, though."

That was the first time anyone had ever told me that. But I wasn't really happy to hear it. I've always believed in my own kindness and correctness. S-so i-it's not like this makes me happy at all, okay?!

"Two truths running counter to each other? Isn't that contradictory? Like Conan always says, 'There is only one truth,'" I said, in an attempt to hide my embarrassment.

"Unfortunately, I'm more into the future boy than the boy detective." Miss Hiratsuka warded off my remark with a cold smile.

How old is she, seriously?

X X X

We finally got into the ramen shop and went to buy food tickets at the vending machine. In the spirit of ladies first, I let Miss Hiratsuka go on ahead of me. When you're going somewhere dangerous or unfamiliar for the first time, you have to let the lady go first to make sure it's safe!

Miss Hiratsuka pushed the *tonkotsu* button with zero hesitation. It was so manly of her, I almost fell in love right there. After making her purchase, she turned back to me, still gripping her wallet. *Come on, hurry up and get out of the way.*

"What do you want?" she asked.

Oh, so she was planning to pay for me. Now I even want to call her "Bro." I was flattered, but I felt like it would be a bad idea to accept. "N-no, I'll pay for myself."

"No need to be polite."

"I'm not trying to be polite. There's just no reason for you to treat me," I said.

Miss Hiratsuka tilted her head curiously. "Hmm? I thought you were a rotten, sleazy guy who'd expect the woman to pay as a matter of course."

What a cruel thing to say. "That would make me a leech! I don't want to be a leech. I want to be a stay-at-home husband!"

"I—I don't understand the difference." Miss Hiratsuka was astonished.

Actually, I don't really understand the difference, either. But *stay-at-home husband* sounds better than *leech*, doesn't it? Besides, it seems unwise for a teacher to buy meals and stuff for a preferred student. Fortune would favor refusing.

I copied Miss Hiratsuka and chose *tonkotsu*, then went up and took the seat next to her at the counter. No sooner had I produced my ticket than she was specifying to the staff the firmness of the noodles. "I'll take it semiraw," she said.

"Oh, then I'll take mine extrafirm," I added. But, like…do women normally do this cool ordering routing at ramen shops?

There's a deep charm to the image of a modern beauty at a ramen shop. Miss Hiratsuka was receiving an unusual amount of attention, but she didn't seem bothered by it as she cheerfully set up the paper apron provided at the counter and scouted out the black pepper, white sesame, leaf mustard, and pickled red ginger. *Whoa, she's getting way too into this.*

The boil time for both our noodles was quite short, so the ramen came right away. Miss Hiratsuka took a set of disposable chopsticks and put her hands together.

"Thanks for the food."

"Thanks for the food."

First, the broth. The film of oil floating on the surface was smooth like white porcelain. You could see the creaminess. The seasonings canceled out the stink of the thick, rich broth that defined

tonkotsu. Next, the noodles. As thick as the soup was, the noodles were thin and straight. The slightly firm texture gave each bite good balance.

"Yeah. This is good." I voiced my simple impression, and then we both slurped our noodles in silence, drinking the broth with relish. The cloud-ear mushrooms and green onions were a beautiful complement, with the texture of a flounder dancing on your tongue.

With about a quarter of the noodles left, Miss Hiratsuka ordered some more and then spoke to me. "About what we discussed earlier..."

"Yeah?"

"About how you're fastidious." When her extra noodles came, she added some leaf mustard. She was smiling. I guess Miss Hiratsuka was getting excited as her customized ramen approached her ideal flavor. "Eventually, I think a time will come when you'll be more tolerant."

"Uh-huh." I gave her a noncommittal reply as I tossed raw garlic into my bowl.

"It's just like ramen." Miss Hiratsuka proudly showed off her completed Shizuka Special and continued. "When I was younger, I thought *tonkotsu* was the ultimate. Fat was true flavor, and I wouldn't accept anything but rich soup. But then you grow, and you learn how to tolerate light salt and soy sauce broths."

"I-isn't that just you getting old?"

"Did you say something?"

"No..." She's *reeeally* glaring at me now...

After a momentary scowl, Miss Hiratsuka caught me off guard with another smile. "Well, whatever. You don't have to tolerate those things right now. If you can one day, that's enough."

I think she understands my conflicts and doubts. But even so, she isn't pointing me toward any concrete answers. Not that I can answer anything right now, anyway.

"Not to say that you'll be able to tolerate everything. I hate tomatoes, so I still can't stand tomato noodles."

"You do?"

"Yeah, I can't stand how squishy they are, and they kinda taste like grass."

What a kid. But I get her point. For people who hate tomatoes, the gooeyness of the flesh and the seedy bits is its own form of torture. It's a little gory-looking, too.

"I hate cucumber for similar reasons," she added.

"I'm not so fond of them, either." Nope, I don't like *kyuuri*. I do like Kiryuu Bannanchiten, though, and Pepsi Ice Cucumber. "Plus, those damn cucumbers sneak into potato salad and sandwiches and make it all taste like cucumber…" I'm okay with them cut into sticks raw or dipped in miso. If they're by themselves, you can avoid them. But the moment you cut them into round slices, that's when they go on the attack… They marinate every single flavorful item in their cucumbery taste. And they're not even that nutritious, either. They're the predators of the vegetable world.

"They're good as pickles, though," noted Miss Hiratsuka. It was something a heavy drinker would say. "I could go for some right now."

I could agree with that. "Yeah, I'd love a few." Yes, indeed. Pickles are good. Very refreshing. Best of all, you can eat piles of rice accompanied by nothing but pickled vegetables. It's heavenly.

"…"

For some reason, the conversation trailed off there, and silence fell upon us. Confused, I looked at Miss Hiratsuka. Had she misheard me or something? She looked totally dazed. When her eyes met mine, she sucked down her water in a sudden panic. "Oh, right, p-pickles. Mm-hmm. M-me too. I…l-love them."

"Uh, it kind of makes me embarrassed when you stammer like that, so please stop."

"…Wh-what are you talking about? More importantly…what was I talking about?"

Is she okay? Maybe she should do some brain exercises right now, like a multiplication sheet. Time for some antiaging magic! All I remember talking about are tomatoes and cucumbers, though.

Miss Hiratsuka's chopsticks moved with nimble cheer. "I'll give you some *char siu*."

"Thanks. Then I'll give you my *menma*."

She chuckled. "Thanks."

"At your age, you need the fiber."

"Part of that sentence was unnecessary."

"Ow!" I rubbed the new bump on my head as I ate.

It seemed Miss Hiratsuka had taken a liking to this ramen. She was smiling with satisfaction. "Now that you've found me such a good shop, though, I feel like I have to show you one, too."

"Any recommendations?"

"Yeah. When I was a student, I knocked out most of the ramen shops in the Chiba city area. But as a teacher, I can't really be going out a lot with a student. I'll show you around once you've graduated."

"Oh, no, I don't need you to come. You can just tell me where it is."

Crack.

The sound of something snapping struck me as particularly loud, even in this busy shop.

"Whoops, I broke my chopsticks."

"Please, I'd love it if you took me..." *I don't think chopsticks usually break in your hands...*

"Mm-hmm. Look forward to it," she said. I think she was the one looking forward to it.

Ramen tastes all right when you're eating it with someone else. It's good when you're alone and with good company.

It's settled: Ramen is the greatest food. You can't convince me otherwise.

Hachiman's mobile
FROM Hachiman 22:51
TITLE Re
Um…
FROM Hachiman 23:25
TITLE Re3
Sorry. This degree of enthusiasm is weirding me out, frankly…

Hachiman and Hiratsuka's mobile chat one day

Hiratsuka's mobile

FROM Hiratsuka 22:43

TITLE None

Thank you very much for today. I was a little surprised to hear that you like ramen. I've eaten my way around the neighborhood, too, so I know a fair amount about local shops. Oh, and that doesn't mean I literally ate the neighborhood. (ha-ha) Now then, I promised we'd go out together once you graduated, but I suspect that if I were to pick a shop close to the school, you would end up going by yourself, so I think I'll take us somewhere farther away. So first let me give you the rundown on places near both the school and your house. If you want a famous ramen shop near the school, the first in line has got to be Tora no Ana. They pride themselves in the outstanding thickness of their broth for Chiba *iekei* ramen. Their noodles would perhaps be considered standard among the Sakai-made noodles and *iekei*, but they are not to be underestimated. There's no *ya* appended to the end of the shop's name, so you can tell the shop is attempting to go in a new direction despite being derived from *iekei*. Their broth is also exceptionally compatible with rice (and pickled vegetables). Rice with seaweed soaked in the broth is utterly divine. I also recommend Shachi, the tsukemen place. And another place for classic Chiba *iekei* would be Masudaya. I'm more acquainted with their Chiba Station shop, but they have a branch in Kaihin-Makuhari, too. While their broth is a *tonkotsu* soy-sauce base, they've figured out a way to distinguish it from regular *iekei* fare. The execution of the marinated eggs and *char siu* in particular arguably ranks second in the region. And in a slight deviation from most ramen shops, they also have Chinese fried rice on the menu. I bet a growing boy like you would enjoy a fried rice and noodle set, Hikigaya. (ha-ha) They serve their *tsukemen* with red bean paste, too, which is quite exciting. And there's one more shop, if you're going toward.

FROM Hiratsuka 23:20

TITLE Re2

I'm sorry. I pressed send before I was done. If you're going toward Tokyo, you can't miss Naritake. I think you know them, too, but they use lots of back fat, ultra-thick noodles, and rich-tasting broth. It has miraculous balance, the holy grail of Chiba ramen. The main branch is in Tsudanuma, but they have shops by Chiba Station and Motoyawata, and recently, they've even expanded into Tokyo with their Kinshi-cho branch. I recommend "oily" when you choose how much grease you want, but I think they also have a "super-oily" option. When you take the *meat* radical and add *delicious* to it, you get *fat*. Truly wise. As for other shops in that area, there's Kaizan and Ichioshi. Though they're both *tonkotsu* base, the flavor of the dashi is distinctly noticeable and strikes an excellent balance with the fat. With the medium-thick straight noodles, it's especially 👍. Their thick slices of *char siu* steeped in that broth are irresistibly satisfying. And last but not least, those green onions! Their flavoring is just amazing—it enhances the crisp texture and essential sweet spiciness of the green onions. Green onions go well with both their ramen and rice-based meals, so if you go there, you have to get something with green onions! Well, that's about it, so do you have any questions or requests?

FROM Hiratsuka 23:29

TITLE Re4

(´ ;ω; `)

5

Komachi Hikigaya considers that one day, her brother may leave.

It was approaching mid-August, about the time when that summer vacation feeling begins to fade. When I counted the days I had left, melancholy washed over me. It gave the words an eerie ring to them as they came out of my mouth, like the ghost in "Bancho Sarayashiki." *August fiiiirst… August seeeecond… I'm short two mooooonths!* Frankly, I wanted about three more months.

I crossed off one more day on the fridge calendar with the dismay of counting down the days until the world was destroyed. If I put a circle on the calendar, that would be *Takoyaki Manto Man*. There were only two weeks of summer vacation left. Hey, did you do a time leap? I put my finger on the calendar one more time to make sure. *Seriously, did I just count it wrong or something?* That's when something crawled up to my feet.

"…What?" I looked down to see the family cat, Kamakura, gazing up at me with displeasure.

We stared at each other for a few seconds. Then Kamakura snorted and flopped down on top of my feet. *You're in the way, dude.* He seemed to be demanding attention.

Come to think of it, Komachi had constantly been with Sablé for the past two or three days. I guess Kamakura wasn't happy about that and was compelled to come to me instead. I sat down on the floor with an *oof* and started giving him some full-body petting. At first, I slowly stroked him from head to tail in the direction of his fur. After a while, he started purring, so I began rubbing around with my fingers like a gentle massage. Kamakura closed his eyes, huffing in pleasure. He seemed pretty tired.

Well, no surprise there. The entire time Sablé had been with us, he had been chasing Kamakura around. Even here at our house, Sablé ran here and there and everywhere with the unbridled restlessness typical of a small dog. And this seemed to have been his first encounter with a cat. Sablé was extremely curious about Kamakura and charged at him as if to say, *Play with me!* And every time, Kamakura would run someplace Sablé couldn't reach, like on top of the fridge or behind a dresser.

And to make it worse, Sablé drew Komachi's attention away from Kamakura by bothering her nonstop with one thing or another, leaving the cat with no choice but to come to me. *Sorry I'm your only option.*

"Well, you know. Just put up with him and let him have his way until the end of the day today… You're the older brother, you know." I gave Kamakura a speech rather like the one I'd received when I was little. I don't know how old Sablé is, but Kamakura has a longer history in the Hikigaya household, so that gives him seniority. Like a younger performer with a longer career might have.

After my attempt at persuasion, Kamakura slapped his tail on the floor: his grudging reply. Sorry.

I continued stroking his fur, smooshing his paws, and fluffing up his tummy. That's when the door to the living room opened.

"Bro! …Oh-ho, what a rare combo."

Hearing my name, I lifted my head to see Komachi with Sablé in her arms. *Hey, how is it rare to see a cat with his master? What are you trying to say here?* "I've got something of an affinity for cats," I said.

"You do come off as kinda feline."

I don't know what she meant by that. Am I really territorial or something? But I deliberately chose to interpret her remark positively. "I suppose. I am indeed the king of beasts."

"Uhhh… Sure, I guess."

"Why suddenly no comment? Don't give me that pitying look. Didn't you know? Male lions don't do any work at all."

"You really are the king of beasts!" she cried.

"Right?" I gave a triumphant snort.

Sablé yipped from Komachi's arms as if in reply. Kamakura snorted a *funsu!* and stood from where he was sprawled over my feet. He yawned wide like a catbus and wandered off. As he took his leave, he swished his tail back and forth just as if he were waving a hand. I watched him go with a hint of a wry smile on my face.

"So did you want something?" I asked, pushing myself to my feet.

Komachi replied with a start as if just remembering what she'd come here for. "Oh! Yeah, yeah. Lend me your phone, Bro."

"All right, but what for?"

"Hmm, well, I heard there's this app called Dog-lingual? You have your dog bark into it, and it tells you how he feels!"

"Huh. So that's a thing?" Sounds handy. They should come up with a Human-lingual. What people say doesn't necessarily reflect what they actually feel, after all.

"Come on, come on!" Komachi urged me, so I picked up the phone I'd left on the table. My fingers slid skillfully along the phone's surface until the download screen opened. Among the listed apps, there was not only Dog-lingual but also a Cat-lingual.

"Oh, get the Cat-lingual while you're at it," said Komachi.

"Righto." I downloaded the Dog-lingual app and the Cat-lingual app as instructed. "Here." I launched Dog-lingual and handed it to Komachi.

She put down the dog and tried out the app immediately. "Come on! Come on, Sablé! Say something!"

"Yip!" (Play with me!)

"Well, I guess that's it." The message displayed in the Dog-lingual app was about what I'd expected. That was a fairly normal doggy desire.

Komachi continued to keep the app turned toward Sablé. Sablé, like his owner, was good at picking up on what other people wanted, I guess, since he diligently barked into the phone.

"Yip!" (Play with me!)

"Yip!" (Play with me!)

"Yip!" (Play with me!)

"Yip!" (Play with me!)

Huh? What's going on? Is this just copy-paste?

"Maybe it's broken, Bro," said Komachi.

"No, I haven't used that phone enough to break it." Maybe I could bark like a dog to test it. If Dog-lingual displayed something else, it would mean the app was working fine. I promptly began howling toward the future.

"Bowwow!" (I do not want to get a job, that I do not!)

Terrifyingly accurate. Not even an expert could translate that so elegantly. "Looks like it isn't broken after all."

"Yeah, you're what's broken here, Bro." Komachi was beyond exasperated; she had nearly given up. She had the enlightened expression of a high monk.

I would like everyone in my family to know that even I am a little hurt when my own flesh and blood looks at me with such warmth.

"...Anyway, he says he wants to play," I said.

"Hmm. I guess he needs to go on a walk, then," she replied.

"Yeah, go on, then." Then I wouldn't have to hear him yipping at me for a while. He's cute, but it's obnoxious when he's running around the house 24/7.

"Then get me the leash. ♪"

"Yeah, yeah." I did as Komachi said, pulling Sablé's leash from the implements Yuigahama had left to us.

"Thanks. Okay, then put it on him. I'll hold him still." Komachi grabbed Sablé and clung to him as if to say, *Leave this to me; you go on ahead!* While she had him still, I attached his leash.

"Okay, is this fine?" I asked, swinging the hand grip back and forth.

Komachi nodded in satisfaction. "Yeah. All right, then let's go walk this dog!" She pointed at the door with her whole arm.

"You're telling me to do it?" I asked.

"More like I'm walking you. If I don't do this, you'll never leave the house."

Well, that's true. They don't call me Hikki for nothing. I let out a deep sigh, emphasizing with my whole body and soul how much I didn't want to go. But Komachi didn't seem to care one whit, prodding me in the back as she urged me.

"Come on, come on. I'll go with you."

X X X

The sun had already descended, and in the wash of ink over the indigo sky, the white moon was drawing its bow. The area I live in is quiet, the sort of residential block with a one-generation-old look you'll find in any city, but you can find a smattering of fields by the river that runs along the main road, and the street is lined with where farmers live and work. A long time ago—when my mother was young, so about thirty years ago, I guess—there were apparently fireflies around here, by the river and fields. In other words, there aren't anymore. Why do the fireflies die so quickly?

As I recalled what she'd told me, I looked out over the paddies, thinking maybe I'd see one.

Something rustled. A passing wind bowed the ears of rice. After a plentiful shower of sun during the day and sucking up water and nutrients from the ground, the rice was full and ripe. It was as if the wind was pushing its way through the field. When I was little, I used to think it looked like the work of something supernatural.

I don't see any fireflies or spirits now.

Why is it that people are so taken in by nostalgia? People claim, *It used to be better* or *The good old days* or *Oh, this reminds me of the Showa era!* The older it is, the more of a positive light people are prone to seeing it in. They think fondly of the past and yearn for olden times, or they lament and mourn what has changed, what has been changed. Doesn't that mean that, fundamentally, change is cause for sadness? Are growth, evolution, and transition really so joyous, right, and wonderful? Even if you don't change, the world and everything around you will. What if everyone is just desperately chasing after the crowd because they don't want to be left behind?

When there is no change, no sadness comes into the world. In my opinion, preventing the birth of something negative has serious advantages, even if it means nothing is born at all. If you check your balance sheet and you're not in the red, then you're heading in the right direction, economically speaking.

That is why I won't rule out the option of never changing. I have absolutely no intention of denying who I was in the past or who I am in the present. Change is, ultimately, about running away from your current situation. If you choose not to run, you should stay the same; you should stand firm right there. There are things to be gained from not changing. It's like how you'll learn moves faster if you cancel evolution with the B button. I answered that question for myself at some point… I feel like it was a long time ago.

Komachi was holding the leash as if she enjoyed the feeling of being tugged along. "Hey, hey, watch out. There's a car." The vehicle skimmed by us.

Sablé snorted and sniffed some grass, then began scarfing it down. Both dogs and cats eat grass like this so they can cough up hairballs, so this is a necessary process on walks. Komachi and I stopped, waiting there for Sablé to finish literally chewing the scenery.

Komachi compared me and Sablé, then gave me a pleased smile. "Man, it's been so long since we last went for a walk together."

"Yeah." It had indeed been quite a while since we had gone out strolling together. I tend to prefer spending my time at home, so unless we have a clear goal like shopping or a pet show, I don't walk around with Komachi very often.

Sablé tugged at the leash, and Komachi smiled at him. "Okeydoke. Let's go." Sablé yipped in response and launched into the characteristic hoppity-hop walk of the miniature dachshund. I followed after them.

So many lights intermingled—the faint afterglow in the western sky, the evenly spaced streetlamps coming on at once, and the sundry lights of each house. In the slowly dimming town, the currents of people flowed in various directions: salarymen heading home, housewives going shopping for dinner, elementary schoolers running alongside their bicycles with friends, middle schoolers chatting at the convenience store on the way back from clubs, high schoolers just going to hang out, and mothers going to pick up their children. The scene was filled with the type of nostalgia and warmth you often take for granted.

"It's a blessing to have someone there to welcome you home," Komachi murmured.

"Yeah, I guess. Not in every single circumstance, though."

"Wow, you really are a killjoy," said Komachi, clearly fed up with me.

But hey, I mean, there are exceptions to every rule. I might be like, *Oh, there's no one here to welcome me home…*, but if some random hippo suddenly showed up to greet me and recommend me some mouthwash, I would not feel blessed at all.

"You may be a killjoy, but I'm still happy when you welcome me home." Komachi looked away from me toward Sablé.

As her pace slackened, I passed by her. I had to have her behind me, or she'd see my face relaxing into a smile. "I don't really do it for you, though. I just happen to be there, okay?" I retorted, embarrassed, and there was the slightest pause.

"Still. It's nice," she said warmly, and without thinking, I turned around. Komachi closed her eyes and put one hand to her chest. As if to confirm the faint but gradually warming heat, she spoke each word slowly. "That just now was Admirable and Noble Little Sister Komachi showing off her cuteness." Her smile was the fakest one I'd seen all summer.

"Uh-huh…" *So obnoxious…* I straightened my shoulders out of their droop and started walking again, leaving Sablé and Komachi behind. *Good grief, she's really not cute when it comes to the important stuff. Usually, she's cute. Supercute.*

Komachi kicked a pebble with the toe of her sandal and gazed up at the flickering stars just beginning to shine. "While you were away in the hospital, Kaa was there for me, anyway. He actually comes to the door for me."

"He doesn't come to the door for me. He just looks down at me from the veranda."

"That's just him being disagreeable to hide how much he cares," Komachi joked, giggling. "It's a rough life being surrounded by you *hinedere* types."

"That again? I'm not secretly soft and caring." In fact, I'm not disagreeable, either. On the contrary, there's no one more upright than me. I just seem twisted despite my respectable life because the world is so warped and distorted.

"Well, it's nice to have someone welcome me home, *hinedere* or not." This time, she was chuckling.

"What? I'm not gonna be around forever. You've gotta let go of your brother's apron strings."

"Huh...? You're gonna move out, Bro?" Komachi stopped in place and turned to look at me. Gone was that manufactured, pasted-on smile. Now, she looked like she'd been shot all of a sudden.

"Of course not. I'd never leave without a reason."

"That's a relief..."

"Living at home is so easy, it's great. I'll take unemployment to the limit. It's just how I roll."

"...or not. I'm anxious about your future..." Komachi held her head in her hands.

I put my hand over hers and gave her head a gentle thump. "I can live at home while I'm going to school, and I plan to pick a university I can commute to. I'm not leaving unless something drastic happens." If I can get into the university in Chiba city, the commute is an hour or so, and that's good enough. Well, if it was the campus in Kanagawa or Tama, I'd have to do some thinking. And Tokorozawa... That place is so remote, I'd need to go in heavily armored.

"I think that's kinda weird for a guy your age. Don't you want to move out at all?"

"Eh, not really," I said. "Our parents are pretty laissez-faire, and they both work, so I get time to myself. There isn't really anything inconvenient about it."

"...Or so he justified it to himself, but in truth, he just didn't want to move out because he'd be too lonely if he lived apart from Komachi."

"What's with the weird monologue?" *Ha-ha-ha, don't be so stupid, ha-ha-ha.* "There's just no benefit in living on my own. It costs money, and I'd have to spend time and effort doing chores. How can you do chores when you don't get anything for it, anyway? Don't you know the principle of equivalent exchange?"

The Hikigaya family isn't on bad terms. Our dad is completely worthless, but really it's just his ideas and everything he says that's garbage. I don't really have any complaints about him aside from that. I've never seriously considered moving out, so in that sense, I have no real desire for independence. Not without reason, anyway. Well, I guess people who live alone must have reasons for what they do.

"Oh, you!" said Komachi. "We all know you're actually *so* lonely!"

"Huh? What is this loneliness you speak of? Is it something you'll go check out, something you'll go find in your neighborhood Akihabara?" I don't experience that kind of emotion. I'm the type who loves his alone time more than anything else, so to me, loneliness is my wonderful something. ♪

"I'd be lonely, though."

She totally ignored my joke. Ngh, I guess it was a little forced! Komachi was dribbling the conversation right past me like a pro soccer player, so I dropped the joke and went with it. "Well, maybe you would be, but I—"

"I'm not just talking about you. I mean, Yukino lives alone, doesn't she? I wonder about her... I wonder if she's okay." She seemed to be implying that perhaps even Yukino Yukinoshita experiences a touch of loneliness in her life. Though Yukinoshita conducted herself in an absolutely perfect manner, she occasionally revealed her fragility. Or perhaps you could call whatever it was a sense of transience. *Not that I understand what that means yet, though.*

"And...," Komachi continued, "I think the people who get left behind feel lonely, too."

...Yeah, that was true. I wonder why I thought the only one who would be lonely is the person who leaves, even though the people left behind would surely feel the same. If Komachi were to get married and move out, I know I'd blubber like a baby.

Komachi tugged the leash to prompt Sablé to get going. I took over the leash as if taking a baton from her.

"Bro?"

"You must be tired. I'll handle it."

She was obviously not going to be tired from walking such a tiny dog. Only an extremely feeble girl would be tired out by that. Komachi gave me a curious look before breaking into a sudden smile. "Yeah, thanks. I'll make sure you don't wander off anywhere," she said, squeezing my hand.

"I said I'm not going anywhere. I'll stay at home until I get married off."

"...Does 'married off' really apply to househusbands, too?"

"Then until I get married on."

"Well, I guess...it doesn't really matter."

It's been so long since we last took this path, and the town has changed from how it used to be. Let's go the long way around and head home.

X X X

Right when dinner was just about ready, the doorbell rang. Komachi was standing in front of a pot on the stove, so I decided to get it instead. I could see Yuigahama on the intercom screen, cheerfully adjusting her hair. I figured she was there to pick up Sablé. Once I'd checked the intercom, I went out to let her in.

When I opened the door, she waved. "Oh, yahallo!"

"'Sup."

"Here's your souvenir," she said, handing me a paper bag.

From the size and weight, it didn't seem to be a wooden sword. Too bad. I would have been rather pleased to receive a keychain of a little sword with some random dragon winding around it or a glow-in-the-dark skull keychain.

"You can only get them there!" she said.

"Huh…"

I looked into the paper bag, as Yuigahama instructed, and inside were sweets from her trip. Well, they were a regional version of snack you'd often see for sale. It was a pretty safe choice. It indicated where she had gone, and she had also been careful to choose something that few people would dislike. The sweets were in individually wrapped packets, so it would be easy to pass around at work or school. It was a very tactful souvenir. But seeing her gift suddenly reminded me of a particular incident. "These are…"

"Huh? You don't like them?" Yuigahama peered into the paper bag in my hands, looking worried.

"No, they're fine, but…girls always buy something like this as a souvenir, don't they? And then they pass them around to all the other girls in class."

"Yeah, that's true. Some people don't, though. Like Yumiko."

Miura, huh? I'd expect nothing less of the queen. She takes it for granted that other people should be the ones buying stuff for her, and I can respect that. "Once, someone put a wrapper from some region-limited snack into my shoe cubby," I said. "It was definitely one of the girls in my class. She clearly had no desire to hide the crime, either. Her confidence just made it hurt all the more…" A dry chuckle welled up in my throat.

Panicking, Yuigahama attempted to amend the situation. "I-it's okay—that's not gonna happen this time!"

"I hope not."

"It'll be fine!" Yuigahama insisted, clenching a fist. "Nobody's even aware of you enough to do something like that."

"That's true." Her comforting skills were practically nonexistent, but she was actually convincing anyway, so whatever. *I'm really glad my stealth abilities have been giving me results. They're so good, they could even work on the Ant King.* I was relieved to hear I would be able to spend the second semester in peace and tranquility.

Yuigahama, however, was peering into the house from the door with a little concern. "So how is Sablé?"

"Oh, he's good," I told her. "Komachi!" I called into the house.

Komachi came to the door, holding Sablé in her arms. He yipped.

When she saw him, Yuigahama smiled. "Thanks, Komachi!"

"It was nothing," my sister replied.

Yuigahama petted the dog in Komachi's arms and asked, "He didn't cause you trouble?"

"Oh, no, not at all," replied Komachi. "We played together with Dog-lingual and stuff. It was fun."

"Dog-lingual? Oh, that thing. I remember they used to have that, a long time ago."

"There's an app out now," I said, but since it would be faster just to actually show her, I launched the program.

"Let me see, let me see." Yuigahama circled around for a better view of my phone, and then to test it out, she tried calling out to her dog. "Come on, Sablé! It's me!"

Sablé tilted his head, looking puzzled. "Waff?" (Who's she?)

"Sablé?!"

The despair in her tone probably startled him, as he yipped and ran around my ankles. I scooped him up in my arms and then gently put him into the carrier Komachi had brought over. I zipped it up and handed it to Yuigahama. "Here. He'll remember you in a couple of days."

"Ngh... I really wanted him to remember..." She was half in tears, but she held the carrier firmly and with care. Sablé pressed his nose against the mesh and whined.

"...See you, then," I said. I hadn't been all that partial to the dog, but now that it was time to part, there was a little something welling up inside me. If he started yipping in protest, then all the more.

"Bring Sablé over again sometime to play, Yui." Komachi, her eyes a little wet, took Yuigahama's hand. She had been glued to our guest for the past three days.

"I will! For sure!"

"Yes, please do," said Komachi. "When our parents are here, with a box of cakes, while you're doing your greetings." Komachi's eyes glinted suspiciously.

"Yeah, greeting your pa… Wait, what?! No! No, I'm not going after all!"

Komachi clicked her tongue quietly, her expression quickly changing back to normal. "Anyway, I hope you do come over again sometime. I'll be waiting."

"Yeah, thanks." Yuigahama expressed her gratitude, then heaved up Sablé and the rest of the doggy things. It was about time for her to go.

And that's when I remembered. "Oh yeah, about Yukinoshita. She might be at the fireworks show. Miss Hiratsuka was saying that since it's a municipal event, a lot of VIPs will be showing up with their families."

"Oh, really? All right. I'll go and check it out." Yuigahama paused for a moment as if something had suddenly occurred to her. She quietly took a deep breath and focused on me. "U-um…s-so do you want to go see the fireworks together? As thanks for taking care of Sablé. I'll buy you some kind of food there."

"You hear that, Komachi? Let's go to the fireworks," I said.

The two of us going alone together had never been an option. Besides, I mean, if this was her thank-you, Komachi should go as the one who had actually been taking care of Sablé.

Komachi apparently saw right through me. She set her hands on her hips and let out a tiny sigh of exasperation. "Good grief," she muttered, "completely useless, as always," but I ignored her. Komachi offered Yuigahama her apologies. "Oh, I'm *really* flattered by your invitation. But I'm so busy studying for exams. I know you want to do something for me, but I don't know if I can go out…"

"Oh...of course."

"Yeah, I'm sorry. *Buuut!* But, but! There's some stuff I'd like you to come help me buy. But, well... Agh, I just don't have the time to go! I really want it, but I don't have the time to go shopping! Whatever shall I do?! It's so much to carry, too, so you'd have some trouble getting it on your own, Yui," Komachi recited with incredibly forced delivery, and then the little twit looked right at me.

Yuigahama realized what that meant and jumped on that opportunity with gusto. "Oh! Y-yeah! Hikki! Why don't you come with me to buy that thank-you gift for Komachi? She's done a lot for you, too, after all!"

"U-uh... Well, um..." I racked my brain for a reply, but Yuigahama was staring straight at me.

I could hear Komachi whispering quietly behind me. "I'd be worried about a girl going all alone to the fireworks show, you know! It's so dangerous out there these days... Oh, if only there were some boy right now who had the time to go..."

"U-um, if you have plans to go with someone, or if you're busy, you...don't...have to, though..." Yuigahama hedged, giving me a timid glance.

When I say I'm doing "nothing much," I'm doing literally nothing. So of course I was also free on the day of the fireworks. Plus, in the face of such an appeal, there was no way I could refuse. The inner and outer moats were already filled in. It was like the summer campaign of the Siege of Osaka.

"Well, since this is for Komachi, too, then. Call me whenever," I said, returning to the living room.

Just before I shut the door, her cheerful reply reached my back. "Yeah, I'll e-mail you later!"

X X X

With Sablé gone, the house was now quiet. It was so still, it was like all that 24/7 yipping had never happened. As I washed the dishes, the clinking rang out clearly. When I turned off the faucet in front of me, I could hear the sound of an insect far away. The Hikigaya household would probably remain in this typically tranquil mood until our parents came home.

From the kitchen, I could see Komachi sinking into the sofa, somehow cheerless as she let out a long sigh. I filled a glass with barley tea pulled from the fridge and handed it to her. "For all your hard work."

She accepted the proffered glass and guzzled it down all in one go, giving a satisfied *ahhh* before returning the glass to me with a grunt. "Man, I'm tired… I feel like I've just sent my child off into the world." Komachi seemed greatly aged, wearing a calm expression that belonged on a granny zoning out on the veranda.

"It's that bad…?"

"But this is Yui, so maybe I can relax and leave it to her…"

"He was never your dog in the first place. Just how shameless can you get…?" I sighed.

Komachi looked up at me, tilting her head. "Huh? Oh, we're talking about Sablé?"

"What? We weren't? Then what were we talking about?"

"Nothing!" On the sofa, Komachi flopped over and rolled around lazily. She reached out to pull a cushion toward her but was prevented by the sleeping Kamakura sprawled out on top of it. The cat seemed more relaxed than usual. He usually slept curled up, but this time he was stretched out with abandon, with one paw stretched over his head, one paw on the chest, and one leg bent like that guy who always went "Sheeeh!" I guess now that Sablé was gone, he could finally let his guard down. His fuzzy tummy was completely exposed and vulnerable. It was the kind of no-guard strategy that would make even Southern Black Panther Ray Sefo reflexively go on the defensive.

When Komachi saw that, her eyes sparkled. "Kaaaa-*yutie*!" She pounced on him, burying her face in his tummy, smooshing his paws so hard they might come off and purring in unison with him. "Oh!

We could ask what he really feels like right now! Bro, Cat-lingual! Hurry up and get it! Come on, come on!"

"A-all right." As instructed, I hurriedly got my phone, launched the app, and immediately handed the phone to Komachi. Komachi thrust it in Kamakura's face.

"Purr, purr, purr." (I'm suffocating… Help… Itchy. Tasty.)

"Kaa?!" Komachi panicked.

Hey, is this cat okay? And is the guy who made this app okay? He's the one who's messed up, isn't he?

After that little incident, Komachi played with Kamakura nonstop as if to stave off her loneliness. Though Sablé hadn't been with us for very long, she had given him a lot of TLC.

Their frolicking made for a charming scene, and after I'd watched them for a little while, Komachi peeked at my phone. "Oh, Bro," she said. "Your battery's running out." She held it out to me.

"Mm-hmm. Okay," I said, accepting it. Indeed, the battery life was down to a few percent. It would run out of juice at any minute. I noticed the tiny clock displayed in the upper corner of the screen—it was getting rather late. "Perfect timing. You should get back to studying."

"Okaaay!" Komachi gave Kamakura one final pet and slid off the couch to leave the living room. She was probably going to study in her own room.

Finally released from Komachi's clutches, Kamakura sauntered up to me just as he had when Sablé had been with us, looking drowsy and tired. *You've been working hard, too.*

While I was hunting for my charger so I could keep my phone on, Kamakura gave a high-pitched mewl. The Cat-lingual app was still running, and it flashed some characters on the screen.

I laughed in spite of myself when I saw it. "Yeah, no kidding."

Kamakura meowed once more in reply, but the screen had already gone dark.

Hachiman's mobile
FROM Hachiman
03:19
TITLE Re
Thanks
FROM Hachiman
03:21
TITLE Re3
You're awake? Go to sleep
FROM Hachiman
03:22
TITLE Re5
Night

Hachiman and Komachi's mobile chat on his birthday (August 8)
Komachi's mobile
FROM Komachi 00:00
TITLE None
Happy Birthday!
FROM Komachi 03:2
TITLE Re2
That delayed-reply attack was mean!
FROM Komachi 03:21
TITLE Re4
((_ _))..zzzZZ

6

And so **Yui Yuigahama** disappears into the throng.

Now and then you'll hear people commenting, *There's no sense of regional community anymore* or *Nobody connects with their neighborhoods these days*. And that is indeed true. This is coming from a guy who doesn't even connect at school, much less the neighborhood, so you can be sure it's true.

I don't really know enough about how it used to be to talk about the good old days, but personally, at least, I've never really felt like part of a regional community. I guess it's because every time I hear about some regional thing, I have no idea who the hell people are talking about. When people bring up the head of the neighborhood association or the mayor or whoever, I can't even call their face to mind. This one time in middle school, they came up with this slogan, "Let's pick up garbage for the community!" and scheduled our entire afternoon block with clean-up activities. But of course, it was hard to give a damn in service of some randos, so I ended up spending the afternoon on a plain old walk.

But there are times we can just barely sense the existence of this "regional community." Days like this one. All afternoon, I had been hearing far-off popping sounds. And then, as if waking from a long sleep, the town reverberated faintly.

When I left the house, I could sense a restlessness and agitation on my skin that seemed to be in cahoots with the strong rays of the summer sun. Walking down toward the station, I saw a lot of people moving in the same direction as I was. The women in *yukata* stood out in particular among the crowd.

On the train, I found myself at the center of clingy couples and families carrying cooler boxes. I stuck my earbuds in and zoned out as I stood there, but I was soon overwhelmed, chased into the corners of the train. It was only a matter of time before my spiritual pressure would disappear.

For the next few minutes, I breathed quietly so as to avoid notice. The train rolled through a few stops, and then finally, my destination would be the next one. When the doors slid open, I was the only one who stepped out of the train—there were far more people going in. After the voice-over announced "The door is closing!" I watched the doors roll away and then dragged myself to the ticket gate.

Good grief... I had this staggering feeling that this was a pointless trip. Just imagining getting on that crowded train again was draining my patience. *Once I see her, I'm gonna give her a piece of my mind*, I thought, nourishing my seed of disgruntlement as I passed through the ticket gate against the flow of the crowd. It was only one minute past our meeting time.

I had assumed she would already be there, but...looking around the area, I couldn't catch a sign of that slowpoke anywhere. I didn't see any Bulbasaurs or Squirtles, either. As I leaned on a pillar in the concourse, I recognized a few passersby from school. Of course, I didn't really know them, so I didn't say anything, and they didn't, either. They were all wearing traditional clothes. As I watched the high school kids, I caught sight of a girl emerging from the north exit, clip-clopping along in her wooden geta sandals.

Little flowers bloomed here and there all over her pale-pink *yukata*, which was decorated with a vibrant crimson obi sash. Her pinkish hair was not in her usual bun but rather pulled up tightly in an updo. She seemed unused to wearing geta. Her footsteps were particularly unsteady as she instinctively took two, three hurried steps forward. "Oh, Hikki! I was in a bit of a rush, and...now I'm late..." Her smile was shy, apologetic, and sort of embarrassed.

"No, it's fine." We were facing each other, but for some reason, we both fell silent. Yuigahama lowered her eyes, smoothing her hair over her head. Are you Hamtaro or what? "Well, um…your *yukata* is nice," I said.

Why am I complimenting her yukata*? You're supposed to compliment what's inside it.*

But Yuigahama seemed to get the idea before I could correct myself. Her eyes darted all around as she replied, "Um…th-thank you."

Silence again. What am I supposed to do here? *The only thing I can think of that's this silent is Seagal.* In an attempt to rescue us from deadlock, I spoke. "…So…let's get going."

"…Yeah." I began to walk, and she clip-clopped behind me.

We passed through the ticket gates and waited for the train coming from Tokyo. Yuigahama was looking at her feet the entire time, not saying a single word. I'm not the type to be bothered by silence. But Yuigahama is. She gets particular over such trivial stuff, and that got me anxious because maybe if I didn't say anything, she'd get angry. I figured I'd just say something, anything, to get things going. "Hey, so why did you want to meet at a random halfway point instead of just meeting up there?"

"Because…it's hard to meet up when there's so many people."

"You have a phone, don't you?"

"It's hard to hear, though."

Oh yeah. Now that she mentioned it, I'd heard it's hard to hear your phone when you're in a crowded place. I've never used a cell phone in a crowd, so I thought that was an urban legend. Not that I use my phone very much in less crowded places, either, though.

"Besides, meeting up there would just be…bland," she said.

"Why would you need it to be flavorful? It's not seaweed."

"Wh-who cares! Do you have a problem with it?"

"No, ma'am." *She got mad at me…*

And so silence fell again. Though it was still completely bright out, we were groping through the darkness, sensing nothing but each other's presence.

"So this fireworks show..."

"About the fireworks show—" We started at the same time.

Flustered, Yuigahama gestured for me to go ahead.

"...So this fireworks show," I asked, "do you usually go?"

"Oh yeah. I go every year with friends." Right as she replied, the train came.

"Huh."

A lot of the people on the train were probably headed out to see the fireworks. Not only were they wearing *yukata*—some were carrying vinyl picnic blankets and parasols. It was pretty packed. But it was just one stop. We stood beside the door. The doors rattled shut, and then the train began to move.

"Were you going to say something before?" I asked.

"Yeah. Um...I was gonna ask...have you ever been to the fireworks?"

What a blindingly trivial question. *"Oh, we were thinking the same thing!" Stop it. Stop that shy little smile. It's catching. It's gonna be a real pandemic.*

I averted my eyes and checked my watch. *Still only four, huh...?* "I went once before when I was in elementary school, with my family."

"Really?" And the conversation cut off again. Our conversation had been cut in so many places, it was practically a tuna. The train continued on. Right about when I caught a glimpse of Port Tower in the distance, we began to brake.

"Eek!" Yuigahama yelped, and I heard the sound of geta clacking as a sweet scent wafted into my nose. A soft weight pressed into my shoulder. Yuigahama had lost her balance—probably because of those sandals she wasn't used to—and had fallen over on me. I caught her automatically.

"..."

"..."

Our faces were incredibly close. She blushed red and quickly backed away. "S-sorry..."

"Hmm. Well, it's crowded..." I turned my head away, pretending to watch the scenery from the window. I breathed a long sigh and hid my face from Yuigahama. Although the moment had passed, I was breaking out in sweat.

M-man, that made me nervous... Phew, that was close. So close. Moments like that could make a regular guy inadvertently fall for her.

But that wasn't going to happen here. I'm not having any more misunderstandings, making any more assumptions, or getting the wrong idea ever again. Trying to find meaning in plain coincidence or mere phenomena is the kind of bad habit you see in guys who can't get girls. When she greets you in the morning, that's just common politeness.

When she drops her handkerchief in front of you, that's carelessness. And when a girl at your part-time job gives you her e-mail address, it's because she wants you to cover her shift. I don't believe in coincidence, fate, or destiny. All you can believe in are company orders.

I really think you shouldn't turn into that kind of adult. I don't wanna get a job...

When we emerged from the station, the area was overflowing with people and abuzz with noise. Port Tower soared over us, reflecting the world below in its mirrored walls and intensifying the light of the sunset. It was as if that light were stirring up the expectations of the crowds even more as they eagerly awaited the start of the show. They were all laughing loudly and exchanging cheery, joyful looks.

There were your standard food stalls like *takoyaki* and *okonomiyaki* all along the way, neighborhood convenience stores and liquor stores lining up their goods outside under their awnings, and restaurants announcing that you could see the fireworks from their shop as they enthusiastically reeled in customers. It was summer in Japan. It must be wired into us at a genetic level, because you can't help but get excited. The Chiba Municipal Fireworks Festival was about to begin.

X X X

The station wasn't too far from the place where they'd be shooting off the fireworks. I'd even say the entire park is adjacent to the station. But the area was jammed with so many people, it was hard going. Normally, the plaza was deserted, giving the area a wide-open feel, but now, even from afar, I could see it was submerged under the waves of people. The air was stuffy, but there was a pleasant sea breeze blowing through.

When I checked the clock, it was still only just after six. I was pretty sure the fireworks were starting around seven thirty. So what to do until then? I turned to Yuigahama beside me and asked, "Looks like we still have some time, so what do you want to do? Go back?"

"I'm not going back! How can you just automatically suggest we go home?!"

That was a bad habit of mine. Whenever I go out, I'm thinking about when I get home. No matter when and where I go, I always prioritize getting back alive—I'd make such a great spy or ninja, it's worrying. "Then what do you want to do?" I asked. I was just about to add, *Go home after all?* when Yuigahama pulled her cell phone out of her drawstring coin purse.

"Umm, well, Komachi sent me an e-mail with a list of the stuff she wanted us to buy." She tapped her phone a few times and then showed it to me. All the sparkling, garish, cumbersome rhinestones on her phone made it an eyesore, but I decided to focus on the screen for the moment.

> Komachi's shopping list
> *Yakisoba*...400 yen.
> Cotton candy...500 yen.
> Ramune...300 yen.
> *Takoyaki*...500 yen.
> Your memories of the fireworks...priceless.

What's with that last line?

Your big brother is imagining you typing this out with a smug look on your face, Komachi, and he's a little embarrassed...

Yuigahama seemed to notice my eye-rolling, as she gave me a strained smile and tittered. *This is humiliating! Your big brother is so ashamed now!*

Man, Komachi strikes again. Nobody asked for your schemes, I thought. Well, I get that she's trying to be helpful in her own way. I'm not so dense that I can't figure out an obvious setup like this.

In fact, I'm on the perceptive side. I'm sensitive, I'm *over*sensitive, and I overreact.

The reason is because about 80 percent of boys in the world harbor feelings about a girl and think, *Maybe she likes me?* That's exactly why you have to be the one to bully yourself. You always have to have that calm and cool person inside you who will shoot you that chilly glare: *Of course not.* I don't trust other people much, but I trust myself less.

I let out a short sigh and tried to change the mood. "Then let's just go get these one by one."

"Okay." Maybe it was because of Komachi's lame e-mail, or maybe the cheer of the festival had gotten to her, but Yuigahama had a bounce in her step as she clip-clopped along in her geta. Even amid the noisy throng, I could hear her footsteps and her humming.

People were still flowing into the plaza. The usual food stalls were lined up everywhere, and each one was packed with customers. I knew all the food was mediocre, but seeing the spread in front of me, illuminated by the light of bare light bulbs, it was more appetizing than I had expected. The glistening sauce and oil on the *yakisoba* made it look exceptionally juicy. So juicy that I thought this was Kabaya.

Yuigahama oohed, too, her eyes sparkling as she tugged at my sleeve. "Hey, hey, what do you want to eat first? Candied apples? How about candied apples?"

"That's not on the list." And since when did our goal become eating and not shopping?

Yuigahama eyed the candied apples before reluctantly turning back to me, her phone in hand. "Then what do you want to get first?"

"First, we'll get the things that aren't temperature sensitive, I guess. So then that means the cotton ca—"

"Oh, wow! You can win a PS3 here!" Just as I was about to walk away, Yuigahama yanked on my sleeve. Her attention was glued to the treasure fishing booth. There was a PS3 and other generous prizes piled up there.

"Come on, you're never going to win that...," I said. "Anyway, just listen to me."

"Huh? But they've got strings attached to them," she said.

"Yeah, they're attached somewhere. Who knows where, though." Each prize had a string attached to it. All the strings were then bunched together before splitting off again in every direction. The customer would have no idea what kind of trick was between the string ends and the prizes. "Listen. Any time they show off all the good stuff like that, it's a trap. If something looks like it's gonna work out in your favor, there's always a catch. That's common sense."

"In what world is that common sense? ...The criminal underworld?"

Our conversation was earning us a glare from the old guy at the treasure fishing booth, so I quietly hurried toward the next stall to escape.

I figured we'd get the cotton candy first. The machine at the cotton candy stand rumbled and vibrated as it disseminated its sweet scent into the air, spinning fluffy white threads and weaving them together. The cotton candy was then stuffed into bags and hung from the awning. All the bags had anime characters or superheroes printed on them—probably making Toei money.

This stuff is the same in every generation. I think it was like this when I was little, too. Yuigahama apparently shared a similar sense of nostalgia, since she was the same age as I was. She was watching the cotton candy tenderly. "Wow, this stuff really takes me back! Hey, which one do you want?"

I pointed to the pink bag in front of me and paid five hundred yen.

Okay, look—I have absolutely no interest in anime for little girls, and I never even watch that stuff, but since Komachi's a girl, um, I thought I should get one of those, uh, P-P-Precue-whatevers? Those.

Yeah. Not that I'm interested. At all. I give so few shits about that stuff, I can't even tell *Jewelpet* and *Pretty Rhythm* apart.

After we got the cotton candy, we bought the Ramune and then the *takoyaki*. "We'll get the *yakisoba* next, I guess?" suggested Yuigahama.

"Yeah. I think it was over that way..."

I spun around to start toward the next stall, and that's when I noticed a girl looking our way. She gave us a tiny wave and approached us. "Oh, it's you, Yui!"

"Oh, Sagamin!" Yuigahama gave her a tiny wave in return and took a few steps toward the other girl. Both of them were doing the exact same thing.

Oh, so this is that mirroring thing, huh? I saw on *Tokumei Research* that emulating another person's gestures is a technique to make them sympathize with you easier.

So...who was this girl?

At times like these, it's best to fade out, to sink into the background. I'll become a tree!

Man, I could really detect a subtle difference in friendliness in the way they called out to each other. Yuigahama's greeting was entirely sincere. The other girl—this Sagamin or whoever—wasn't entirely friendly, but she was like, *We're close enough not to be acting distant, right?*

So yeah, anyway, who was this chick?

I guess the girl was thinking the same thing as I was, if her questioning look was any indication. "Um..."

"Oh!" said Yuigahama. "Yeah, of course. This is Hikigaya. He's in our class. Hikigaya, this is Minami Sagami, also in our class."

Huh. So we're in the same class? Now that I think of it, I might've seen her before.

Sagami gave a faint, casual bow, and that's when our eyes met.

It was just a flash.

For a fleeting moment, a smile appeared on her face.

"Oh, really! You guys came together, huh? It's been an all-girls fireworks show for me. So jealous! I bet you're having a great time..."

Yuigahama seemed unsure how to respond, but she played along and laughed anyway. "Why are you making it sound like the *All-Girls Swimming Show*? And it's really not like that with us."

But I didn't feel like laughing at all. I was well acquainted with the smile on Sagami's face just then. It had been neither a grin nor a guffaw. It had been an undeniable sneer. She'd taken one look at the guy Yui Yuigahama was out with and clearly scoffed.

"Huh? Why not?" said Sagami. "It's summertime! That sort of thing is nice." The smile on her lips was unfaltering as she briefly scanned me for an evaluation.

That single act froze my heart so cold it was as if that earlier warmth had never been.

And when my heart cools, so does my head. My thoughts became clear and crisp, as if liquid nitrogen were trickling down my spine. My reason and logic and experience all joined forces and faced off against my emotions. It took no time whatsoever for them to reach their verdict, and I easily wrestled my feelings into submission.

I had been about to make another mistake.

Minami Sagami and I have nothing to do with each other. We don't really know each other. And what is the fastest way to understand someone you don't know well?

Label them.

All she has to go on is my social status. And I'm not just talking about Sagami. Everyone does this. Before you get to know someone personally, first you make a guess about them based purely on their associations with certain groups and places and the ranks and titles they hold. It's very common to judge someone as a person based on their school or your job.

You don't hear much about it recently, but an extreme example is the plausible rumors of academic-background filters during job-hunting season.

Yuigahama is a border-transgressing individual with strong communication skills, so I'm prone to forgetting that she's fundamentally a member of the highest caste in our class and our school. I, on the other hand, am at the bottom. Yukinoshita was something else altogether—she was positioned outside the school caste system, but from the perspective of a neutral party, any interaction between Yuigahama and me would seem like nothing more than charity on her part.

I've really made things awkward here… I knew all the teens in the neighborhood would be coming out for a big fireworks event like this. I hadn't thought this through.

You could describe this event as a sort of social networking opportunity for ladies. The boy she brings along could be considered a kind of status symbol, just like how one could measure a girl's value based on the bag she carries or the brand of clothing she wears. For example, if Yuigahama were here with Hayama instead of me, I bet everyone would be reacting totally differently. She'd be invited to the victory interviews tonight. But coming with me, she was basically getting a court-martial and trial in absentia.

I don't believe we live in different worlds. This would feel so much easier if we did. We've both got one foot in the same world, and that's what makes it such a pain in the ass.

I'm okay no matter how much people sneer at me, but I'd feel bad turning Yuigahama into an object of ridicule, too. "It looks like there's a line for the *yakisoba*. I'm gonna go wait over there."

"Oh yeah. I'll be there soon," Yuigahama replied with a somewhat apologetic smile. She stayed where she was, and I quickly left.

Anything that would earn Yuigahama scorn, however small, should be quickly jettisoned. I could hear Yuigahama and Sagami continuing their conversation behind me, but I wasn't listening as I walked away.

I found my way to the *yakisoba* stall, relying only on a brief memory of its location and the scent of sauce. The sight of the stir-fried noodles in the transparent plastic containers held shut by elastic bands and lit by the warm-colored glow of the bare light bulb made me weirdly hungry. I paid for the *yakisoba* and took a container, and that's when Yuigahama showed up.

"Sorry," she said, looking a little awkward.

But she had nothing to apologize for, so I didn't quite know how to respond. "The candied apples," I muttered.

"Huh?" Yuigahama blinked.

"You wanted to get one, right?" I reminded her.

"Y-yeah! I do, yeah! I'll give you half, too!"

"I don't want any." Well, um, uh, if you could cut it in half precisely with a knife or something, then I suppose I'd be okay with that, like, you know…

Anyway, now I was fairly sure we had bought everything on the list. It was right about time for the fireworks to start. I didn't have to look at the clock to tell—the stirring of the crowd told me.

X X X

The sun finally sank into Tokyo Bay, and the heavens were filled with indigo-blue darkness. The moon rose high as if eagerly anticipating the fireworks that would be launched toward it. We made our way from the road lined with food stands to the main venue, where the plaza was already overflowing with people. Plastic picnic blankets covered every square inch of ground as people shared preliminary drinks. From far away, I heard a child crying, and immediately afterward, a nearby exchange of angry bellows.

All that meant there was nowhere to sit or go. If I had been alone, I would have been able to manage. I could have sat wherever or gone farther away to watch the fireworks. But with Yuigahama along, it was another matter entirely. We obviously couldn't be standing for the whole thing, so I decided to look for a place where the two of us could sit. But we didn't even have any newspapers to sit on, never mind plastic blankets. Yuigahama was in a *yukata*, so she probably wouldn't want to sit straight on the ground. *Maybe a nearby bench?* I thought, but apparently everyone else had been thinking the same thing, as the benches were already occupied.

Oh, hey, we have nowhere to go, just like me at a school event.

"Man, it sure is crowded," Yuigahama said with an awkward *ta-ha-ha*.

Yes, indeed. "If I'd known it'd be this crowded, I would've at least brought a little plastic sheet," I said.

"N-ngh… That kinda makes it my fault. Sorry, I should have told you."

"…That's not what I meant. I'm just not used to this stuff. I wasn't thinking that far ahead. Sorry." If I had spared it a little more thought, I could have predicted this. I was a little weary of my own carelessness.

A guy who actually gets girls would probably have thoroughly prepared everything and given her the attention she deserves. Gently taking the lead is more important than being good-looking or whatever. You know, sending sincere e-mails, looking up stuff before you go out together, or taking her mind off things with snappy conversation when you have to wait in a long line.

…Man, what the hell? That all sounds really hard. If you have to do all that to get girls, then I'm fine going without, seriously. And, like, why is it always the guy doing all the work? What happened to gender equality? …Hey! Why do they call it being a "player" when it's actually nothing but work? Wow, that joke was stupid. But my knack for those is one of my favorite things about myself.

Anyway. I think forcing yourself to keep up appearances and putting up this identity that isn't yours, a mask you don't wear when you're alone, is phony. If you have to do all that stuff to get someone to love you, then can you really say they love you and who you really are? Once you change yourself to win affection, to win love, I don't even know if you can still call you *you*. If you've built your relationship on pretense and lies, it'll probably fail in some way or another, and if you've fundamentally changed yourself, then it's not really you.

These trivial musings brought a small sigh from my lips. My eyes had been drifting downward, and as I made a conscious effort to raise them again, they met Yuigahama's as she stood there stupidly with her mouth hanging open. "What…?" I asked.

"…So you *can* be considerate."

"Huh? Don't be stupid. Of course I can. When I sit quietly in the corner so as not to bother anyone, that's me being considerate." I don't talk to people, I walk one step behind others instead of walking abreast, and I never invite anyone out so as not to interfere with their plans. I'm so mindful, I'm practically in a state of permanent meditation.

Yuigahama laughed. "That's not the kind of thing I mean. Um, I mean, like, you're nice? Sorta."

"Oh-ho, so you've noticed. Yes indeed, I am nice. It is because though I have suffered many wrongs, I have always turned a blind eye to everyone and everything, renouncing revenge. If I were a regular individual, the world would be over by now. I'm like Jesus, in a way."

"A regular person can't destroy the world! And regular people don't suffer many wrongs!"

Damn, that was a sincere reply. "Well, whatever. Anyway, there might a space over there. Let's go take a look," I said.

"Okay."

We began to proceed, but only moments previously a rush had begun toward the food stands and the bathrooms, so we were forced to swim against the current as we moved forward. I weaved through the spaces between the masses of people jumbled together. It's a habit of mine to walk without making a sound.

Once I find a gap to squeeze through, a little crowd like this is nothing for me. I'm a star player on par with the Japan National Soccer Team. Ha! I'm an expert at going against the flow. I mean, the world is always leaving me behind, so I'm constantly struggling upstream.

I slipped through the waves of people coming at me like I was dodging wooden men to become a Shaolin monk, eventually coming out to an area where the tide of people began to slow. But then I realized Yuigahama might not have been able to keep up. *Oh man, my skills led me too far ahead, huh?* I thought and turned back, but it turned out there was no problem.

Yuigahama sprinkled apologies of "Pardon!" and "Sorry!" and "Excuse me!" here and there as she slipped and knifehanded through the crowd.

Whoa, she's got a knack for keeping tabs on her surroundings...

"What's wrong?" She caught up to me easily, tilting her head with a questioning noise.

"Nothing." Now that I think about it, someone who is used to crowds like this would obviously be better at handling them. It was apparently not Stealth Hikki's game. "It looks like here is less crowded."

"This is the toll section," said Yuigahama.

Looking around, I saw that there was indeed a black-and-yellow rope clearly cordoning off the area. The entire clearing was encircled by trees, so normally it would be a bit hard to see the fireworks from there. But the toll area was on the top of a small hill, making the view exceptionally good. They seemed serious about security, too. I could see part-timers loitering and circling the area. If we stayed standing here, they would probably drive us away. "I guess we can look some more," I said. The traffic was a little milder when we hugged the rope, so I prompted Yuigahama to follow and began walking.

"Huh? Is that you, Hikigaya?"

The blackness of the night made a striking contrast with the dark-blue cloth of her refined-looking *yukata*; its pattern of giant lilies and autumn grass lent its wearer a chaste appearance.

Sitting there was Haruno Yukinoshita.

The rope drew a literal line between our position and hers in the special section. With the people around her at her beck and call, the chair she sat on was like a throne, and she was the picture of an empress.

X X X

At 7:40, ten minutes after the scheduled time, they broadcast an announcement declaring that the fireworks were now to begin. A smattering of applause went up from the crowd, and someone got excited enough to let out a piercing whistle. If he had been nearby, I might have punched him. I get the impression that about 50 percent of the guys who whistle arrogantly like that are actually the quiet type, and it's only times like these when they cause a racket.

The paid section was on the highest part of the hill within this open area, and it was also directly in front of where they'd be launching the fireworks, so you'd be able to see the show without the trees around obstructing your view. Technically, you had to buy a ticket to get in, but Haruno gestured for us to enter.

"I'm representing my father, you see, so I've had to greet so many people. I was getting bored. I'm glad to see you here, Hikigaya!"

"Huh. So you're the representative. Wow." I basically ignored the latter half of what she had said as my eyes darted around.

Haruno chuckled. "I guess these are what you call VIP seats. You wouldn't be able to get in, normally." She bragged with the innocence of a child. Sometimes unconcealed pride doesn't come off as arrogant.

Haruno Yukinoshita has such a straightforward nature, and I think that's part of what makes her so charismatic. All she had to say was "Sorry, my friends were late," and the people who had clustered around her immediately backed away. What's more, even when she beckoned us into the VIP area, the part-time guards didn't seem to see anything out of the ordinary about it. They didn't come over to check what was going on, not even once. Real VIPs are pretty amazing.

"You're a celebrity…" Yuigahama breathed a sigh that rode the fine line between admiration and shock.

Haruno giggled. "Well, you know my father's job, right? He's got a lot of clout at municipal events like this."

"Prefectural assembly has clout, even in the city?" I asked.

"Oh, you're sharp. I'd expect nothing less from you. But I'd say it's less because of the prefectural assembly and more because of the company."

I think her family does construction or something. If their business includes some public works stuff, well, I bet they would have clout. There have always been three things that are important to get elected, the so-called 3 F's: a foundation of public support, a figurehead, and full bags, and I'd say she's got all three. And for your information, "full bags" basically means cash. You could also call it "for kickback." And by the way, the three most important bags are plastic bags, the bags under your eyes, and my old bag. Hey, what are you implying about my mom?

While the mayor or whoever it was expounded at length upon his gratitude for all parties concerned and made his congratulations and whatnot, Haruno offered us seats next to her own. Yuigahama and I decided to gratefully take her up on her offer. Bowing to her, we both sat down.

I would have leaned back and relaxed, but with Haruno beside me, I couldn't. It wasn't just nervousness because she was a pretty older girl—what I was really scared of was her all-too-perfect outer mask. I got the feeling that something dark was surging within her, and I'm not good at dealing with that sort of thing.

All of a sudden, she leaned right against my ear and whispered into it. "By the way…I'm not impressed to see you playing around with another girl."

"Um, I'm not playing around…"

Her expression immediately turned frigid. "So then you're serious about her, huh? That's even worse."

"Ow, ow, ow!" She tugged my ear just like Sazae does to Katsuo. I escaped quickly, so she didn't damage it too badly, but if she had pulled it a little harder, I might have gone and ended up inviting Nakajima to play baseball with me. "We aren't serious, either…," I said. *What the hell, man, I can't handle pain.* I am not playing the field, nor have I reached any bases with either of them. There will be no home runs but no strikeouts, either. I'm sitting on the bench, thank you very much, so whatever she wants me to say, it's not gonna happen.

Right as I deflected Haruno's attack, the bigwig on the loudspeaker finished his announcements, and finally, the first of the fireworks was to be launched. An extralarge cluster bloomed into enormous flowers in the night sky to musical accompaniment. Layer upon layer of red, yellow, and orange lights spread out in the sky without pause, continuously lighting the darkness.

"Ooh..."

The flowering halos were beautifully reflected in the half-mirror glass of the Port Tower, brightening the night. This was to be the beginning of eight thousand shots of continuous technicolor fireworks. They boomed and popped with a *do-don-PA!* again and again. There were so many *dodonpa*s, I was like, are you Mercenary Tao or what?

Amid the ringing sounds of bursting fireworks, Haruno's chair creaked as she settled deeper into it.

"U-um..." Yuigahama began to speak to Haruno, with me between the both of them. She'd probably been looking for the right moment.

Haruno blinked her big eyes. "Um...Something-gahama, was it?"

"I-it's Yuigahama."

"Oh yeah. Sorry, sorry." Though I could sense absolutely no malice in her, that flub had definitely been deliberate. Haruno was not the type to forget names so easily. I mean, this was a character who rivaled Yukino Yukinoshita... No, Haruno most likely surpassed her. I couldn't suppress my suspicion that that little slip of the tongue was meant to accomplish something. When I gave her a long, hard look to try to divine what it might be, she giggled. A shiver went down my spine. It was like her smile was flaunting her ability to read me like a book. It was its beauty that made it scary.

"Yukinon isn't with you today?" asked Yuigahama.

"I think Yukino-chan's at home," said Haruno. "Public appearances are my job, after all. I told you I'm my father's representative, didn't I? I didn't exactly come here for fun." Haruno jabbed a finger at herself as she gave a jocular grin. "Coming out to occasions like these is my job as the eldest daughter. That's always been my mother's policy."

I seemed to remember that the younger sister had said something similar…that it was Haruno's role to be the public face, and that she herself was only a substitute. I figured that meant Haruno was their father's official successor. Well, I feel like it's extremely reasonable to designate your eldest child as your successor. But that alone was not enough of an explanation.

"Does that mean that Yukinon isn't allowed to come?" asked Yuigahama.

Sure, it was fine that Haruno was the successor. But that didn't explain why Yukinoshita couldn't be here.

Haruno gave something of a troubled smile. "Hmm, well… that's what our mother wants. Besides, it's better to keep things nice and clear, right?"

"Well, you two do look alike," said Yuigahama. "So if only one of you is here, then people wouldn't get you guys mixed up."

I didn't think that was it, though. It was basically an issue of appearances. Doing this to emphasize that there is only one successor prevents unnecessary squabbles. Any apparent disputes between potential successors would most likely be to their disadvantage. Man, it's like a samurai family.

Haruno put her finger to her cheek and breathed a small, uneasy sigh. "You know, our mother has a strong personality, and she's scary."

"Huh?" I said. "You mean scarier than Yukinoshita?"

"Yukino-chan? Scary?" Haruno stared at me and then burst into pleasant laughter. It was melodious in a way her previous chuckles had not been, as if she sincerely found my statement hilarious. Wiping tears from the corners of her eyes, she let out a satisfied sigh. I guess she was concerned about appearances, though, as she cleared her throat. "Geez, that's rude, Hikigaya. She's such a cute girl, and that's what you think of her?" She giggled for a bit longer and then brought her face right close to mine and whispered into my ear. "Our mother is even scarier than I am."

"...Is she human?" I asked. To be not only scarier than the younger sister, but also the elder—isn't that a little crazy? That's beyond a fortified armor shell; that's basically a Gundam.

"Our mother is the type of person who will decide everything for you and then try to make you fall in line, so we have no choice but to try to compromise with her, but...Yukino-chan's skills in that area are rather subpar."

No, she's beyond subpar. You need more subs to be extra clear: sub-sub-subpar.

"So I was rather surprised when she said she wanted to live alone once she started high school," said Haruno.

"So Yukinon moved out when she started high school?" asked Yuigahama.

"Yep, yep. She wasn't the sort of girl to make many demands, so our dad gladly gave her the apartment building."

Man, I wonder why it is that dads of the world are easy on their daughters?

"Our mother resisted it to the bitter end, though," Haruno continued. "She still hasn't accepted the idea..."

"So Yukinoshita is close to your father, huh?" I said.

"Oh-ho, you have interest in your father-in-law?" Haruno joked.

"Please, we both know interest rates in Japan are at an all-time low," I replied.

"Hmm...twelve points."

For someone with such soft features, she sure grades hard.

"It's not quite that they're close. I think it's just that our mother has a strong personality, so our father ends up being the one to patch things up."

I guess it's something like good cop/bad cop. Or more simply, like the carrot and the stick, I guess.

"Though both me and Yukino-chan know that, so it all evens out," she continued.

"What a horrible pair of sisters...," I said wearily.

But Haruno's beautiful smile did not falter as she turned to speak to Yuigahama. "So was this a date? If so, I'm sorry for interrupting you."

"N-no, i-it's nothing like that," Yuigahama stuttered.

Haruno's gaze overlooked nothing as she surveyed Yuigahama. "Hmph… You're acting suspiciously embarrassed. But if it was a date…" Her tone was teasing. There was a momentary pause in the fireworks, so it was dark all around us, and I couldn't see Haruno's eyes. But I was sure there was a glint in them, darker than the night sky.

"…yet again, she wasn't the one."

Fireworks roared up, crackling over Haruno's murmur. The booms continued intermittently, and the sky flickered. The smell of gunpowder wafted toward us, carried on the wind along with the lingering afterimages of lights on the black screen of night. The fireworks occasionally illuminated Haruno's calm smile.

"Um, did you…?" Yuigahama began to speak just as the fireworks shot up.

Haruno erupted into a particularly animated display of excitement and then spun around to face Yuigahama. "Hmm? What was that?" She grinned as if she had been so engrossed in the fireworks that she hadn't noticed anything else.

"Uh, oh, um…it's nothing." Yuigahama swallowed her words, and the conversation ended there.

I could hear the brief cracking of signal guns ringing out, and then there were lights exploding and sprinkling down through the sky. Haruno clapped her hands lightly in the most innocent-looking gesture. *You'd never see her younger sister doing that…* I don't know, maybe Haruno had a natural understanding of how others see that gesture, and that's why she was doing it.

The two sisters looked alike, but at the core, they were so different. Still, it felt like they were both looking in the same direction. It was a little odd.

"Um, Yukinoshita…" I didn't know what to call Haruno, so I just called her by her last name. I had no intention of acting familiar with her enough to call her by her first name. But when I did, Haruno smiled broadly.

"Hmm? Oh, you can call me Haruno, okay? Or Big Sis. In fact, I'd like you to call me that."

"Ha-ha-ha..." A dry laugh slipped out of me. No way in hell. "...Yukinoshita," I continued.

She laughed. "You're kind of stubborn. It's cute."

Damn it, I really don't like this woman... The scariest part was that she was just a little bit older. With someone as old as Miss Hiratsuka, I can compartmentalize her as a full-fledged adult and a completely different entity. But with someone who is only two or three years older, there's a subtly different culture. "You used to go to our school, right, Yukinoshita?" I asked.

"Hmm," she replied. "Yep, sure did. I'm three years older than you," she said in an informal tone.

Yuigahama nodded with an interested *ooh*. "Then are you twenty, Yukinon's sister?"

"Close. I'm still nineteen. My birthday is superlate in the year. Also, you can call me Haruno... 'Yukinon's sister' is too long. If you want, you can call me Harunon. ♪"

Harunon? That sounds like a name for one of those disposable adhesive hot pads.

That brought a strained smile from Yuigahama. "S-so then, Haruno..."

The show was already shifting into the next segment. As the music blared, the fireworks launched into heart shapes and stuff, like they were going for a specific idea. The show went on, sometimes energetic, occasionally more subdued, accompanied by classical music and some songs I didn't know at all, like some recent hits or something.

The pyrotechnicians started firing fewer shots, and it looked like they were going to slow it down for a while. Here and there I caught sight of people getting up to go to the bathroom or to go buy stuff. From where we sat in the paid area, I could hear a multitude of voices

engaged in pleasant chatter. There was a light meal prepared for us on the table—just what you'd expect from VIP seating.

Yuigahama and Haruno entertained themselves with conversation as I sat sandwiched between them. "So that means you're in university, Haruno?" asked Yuigahama.

"Yep. It's a national tech university in the city."

"Whoah… You must be so smart… You're Yukinon's big sister all right." Yuigahama sounded surprised and impressed.

"I actually wanted to aim a little higher, but this was what my parents wanted." Haruno's smile was a mixture of emotions.

Mm-hmm. So if she wanted to work for the local family business, she'd have to go to a local university—was that the idea?

But man, you know…whenever I'm in a group of three or more and people are talking, it's like a given that I'm not a part of it. I feel like I haven't been opening my mouth at all for a while now except to eat. At times like these, the best way to get through it is focus on the food. These noodles are great, really. Yep, this sauce is indeed a boy flavor.

"So, wow, both of you are going for science, huh?" Yuigahama's comment was brief and nonchalant.

Haruno faltered midgesture. The loud fireworks booming in the background highlighted the odd silence beside me as particularly curious. "Yeah. Yuki wants to go to a national science university…" Something in her smile was almost scornful. Maybe it was just me, since I tend to read too deeply into things when it comes to Haruno Yukinoshita. Maybe Haruno really does feel something warm toward her sister.

Yuigahama was silent, watching that smile.

"It hasn't changed, all this time…," said Haruno. "We always match, and she gets the hand-me-downs…" She had a nostalgic, faraway look in her eyes, and her tone was kind. But I was unsettled by how she said it.

I do have a bad habit of reading negativity into everything. But I hadn't been the only one to pick up on it. Yuigahama's hands were clenched into fists on her knees, and they were trembling just a little bit. "Um..."

"Yeah?"

Though Yuigahama's expression made her misgivings clear, Haruno tilted her head in response, utterly composed.

"Do you...not get along with Yukinon?"

"Aw, of course we get along! I love Yukino-chan," Haruno answered instantly, without even taking the time to think, and then broke into a warm smile. The reply and the expression were both perfectly timed and unfaltering. That was precisely what gave me the impression that she had foreseen that line of attack, and her response was merely a counter. Haruno uncrossed her legs, crossed them again in the other direction, and then continued, unaffected. "She's my little sister. She's always been chasing after me. How could she not be cute?"

Always been chasing after me, huh? Should I take that to mean Haruno has continually outdone her sister? There was cruelty in that remark, the cruelty of an absolute winner laughing at a foolish challenger, as if she were dealing with a child.

With no trace of callousness in her perfect, beautiful face, Haruno smiled at Yuigahama. "What about you, Yuigahama? Do you like her?" she inquired.

Yuigahama seemed rather taken aback by the direct question. But still, she did her best to string the words together despite her stammering. "I—I do like her! She's cool, and sincere, and reliable, but it's cute when she occasionally does something really stupid, and she just looks adorable when she's sleepy... And...she's hard to understand, but she's nice, um, and...and...ah...ah-ha-ha. I'm really just running my mouth here." Yuigahama was smiling shyly, the fireworks illuminating her cheeks.

"Oh?" said Haruno. "Well, that's good to hear." For the very briefest moment, her expression was something you could call kind. It was an odd look for her. But I should say—and as you could expect—in the next moment, those eyes turned demonic. "Everyone says that at first. Still, in the end, they're all the same. They get jealous, they reject her, and they ostracize her... I hope you're different." Her smile was so pleasant and so lovely as to be lurid and terrifying.

"...I..." Overwhelmed, Yuigahama was briefly unable to speak. "...wouldn't do that." She did not avert her eyes, staring hard right back at Haruno.

Haruno shrugged and then glanced at me. "You understand what I'm trying to say, right, Hikigaya?"

"Yeah, I guess." *Of course I get it. I've seen it plenty of times already, and not just to Yukinoshita.* Exceptional individuals are eliminated from any group. The nail that sticks up does not just get hammered down. It gets pulled out and thrown away. It gets ignored, exposed to the blustering elements, and then it rots away.

"Yeah, you got it. I like that look in your eyes," said Haruno, and I turned toward her.

Our eyes met, and hers were so cold they made me shiver.

She suddenly giggled. "I really do like you. You have this weird understanding of things, and it's made you all resigned."

That didn't feel like a compliment at all. The implications there were so obvious, and there was no misunderstanding her intent at all. When people make selective compliments, like when people pull out one specific thing to say they like it, you can't trust what they're saying. *I really like your taste!* and *I like that. Oh, and your taste...* are two completely different things. Source: me in middle school. I'm not going to fall for any descriptive trickery now.

"So what about you, Hikigaya?" Haruno asked. "Do you like Yukino-chan?"

"My mother always said to me, *I don't care if you like it or not—just eat it!* So I keep my likes and dislikes to myself," I replied.

Haruno gave me a pleasant smile.

The night wore on, and we watched the fireworks in silence. Golden curtains fell through the sky. When the shower of colored sparks decorated the final moment of the show, we sent them off with a grand applause.

"Well, it's over. I'm going to leave before it gets too crowded." Haruno remarked, standing up. *How about you?* she silently asked.

Yuigahama took the hint and followed suit, standing and turning to me. "Let's go, too."

"Yeah." Just imagining being caught in the crush of people, unable to move, made every hair on my body stand on end. It was probably a good idea to follow Haruno out and leave as soon as possible.

Without any further comment, the three of us began to walk down the path by the toll section that connected to the parking lot. It looked like we could avoid the crowds if we took this way out.

When we arrived at the parking lot, a black rental limo rolled up toward us. I don't know if Haruno had called for it or if first-class drivers are just always one step ahead when they show up, but the limo came alongside the sidewalk where we were walking.

"I can take you guys home, if you like," Haruno offered.

"U-um..." Yuigahama glanced my way, leaving the decision to me.

I didn't reply as I stared at the limo—at this very familiar vehicle. I doubted I was mistaken.

"You can look all you want, but you can't see the scratches anymore."

Haruno giggled. But neither I nor Yuigahama made so much as a twitch of a smile. I guess our silence bewildered Haruno, as her expression tightened as well. "H-huh? So Yukino-chan didn't tell you? I guess I shouldn't have said that." She sounded apologetic. She didn't seem to be lying, but still, the atmosphere was heavy.

"Then...she really..." Yuigahama's voice was so quiet, I could barely catch it.

Even I could easily deduce the rest of that sentence. Then she really did know. Yukinoshita did know.

Our reaction must have startled Haruno, as she attempted to smooth things over. "Oh, but don't misunderstand. She didn't do anything wrong."

Well, yeah...I know that. Yukinoshita has never done anything wrong. To be always right is to be Yukino Yukinoshita.

"She was just in the car. None of it was her fault. You get that, Hikigaya?" she pressed.

This was the first time I'd even heard all this, but ultimately, that changed nothing. It didn't matter how Yukinoshita had been involved; the facts of the matter were concrete. "Yeah. Well, she's not the one who caused the accident, so she had nothing to do with it." My voice sounded colder than I had thought it would. It was a tropical night, but it felt as if my body temperature had plummeted.

There was a sound of tapping sandals, and I sensed a presence one step closer to me. At the silent urging, I forced myself to be a little warmer. "And it's all in the past, anyway! Don't look back—that's what I always say. I mean, constantly thinking about the past is enough to convince you that life is devoid of hope..." *H-hey, the chill came back at the end there! Past trauma is a force to be reckoned with.*

"Oh? Well, if it's all in the past, then all right." Haruno made an exaggerated show of putting her hand to her chest, relief on her face. Perhaps that was why the air between us softened just a bit.

"...I'm going home, then."

"Yeah, gotcha," she replied, making no particular move to stop me. I was easily released.

The driver, sensing the conversation was over, came around to open the door. Haruno gave him a quiet "Thank you" and slid right into the car. "See you later then, Hikigaya." Her wave was quite cheerful. But I didn't really want to see her again, if possible.

The driver closed the door and quickly returned to his seat, and the car began to roll out.

Yuigahama and I set forth in silence. Perhaps we both wanted a little more time to put everything into words.

X X X

We had left the venue early, but apparently, everyone else had been thinking the exact same thing. The station was pretty crowded. The train arrived at the platform a little late, perhaps because of the fireworks show. When we got on, it was just crowded enough that we couldn't sit down, so Yuigahama and I stood in front of the doors. It was one stop until the one nearest Yuigahama's apartment, and three stops until mine—not that far. In less than five minutes, the announcement let us know that the train was arriving at the next station.

We had stayed entirely silent thus far, but then Yuigahama muttered just one word. "...Hey..." When I replied with a glance and a little sigh, she paused for a moment and asked, "Did Yukinon...tell you about it?" It was one of those questions where you already know the answer.

"No, she didn't."

"Oh... U-um...oh!" With a jolt, the train's jostling stopped. The doors opened, and stuffy night air wafted into the train. Yuigahama looked at me and then out the doors, clearly considering what she should do. But immediately the bell rang to announce the closing doors, so she had practically no time to think or deliberate. I sighed and stepped off the train.

Yuigahama exited after me. "Are you okay getting off here?" she asked, a bit surprised.

"It wouldn't feel right to end the conversation there, would it? Did you time that on purpose or something?"

"N-no! It was just hard to say!" Her panicked defense convinced me...

That schemer. Yuigahama is totally a schemer. "...I'll walk you back," I said.

"Thanks..." She murmured her gratitude.

Apparently, Yuigahama's apartment wasn't far from the station. But since she wasn't used to wearing geta, she was walking a little slow. The sound of our leisurely paced footsteps punctuated the quiet night in the town. As the darkness grew deeper, a breeze swept by. Even walking around outside as we were, the heat and humidity didn't feel so bad.

"Did you hear from her?" I asked, continuing our earlier conversation.

Yuigahama weakly shook her head. "You know, though, I think there are just some things you can't say. When the right moment's passed, you just can't. I was like that, too."

That was true. It had taken Yuigahama a whole year to mention the accident, and she had only confessed because I had found out about it.

"You think to yourself, 'I'll do it once I feel ready,' 'I just have to think a little more about it and then I'll do it,' and then you just keep putting it off."

Yeah, I think I kinda understand that. It's really easy to end up in that situation when you have to say something formal. If it's an apology or confession of guilt, even more so. The longer you wait to say something that would be difficult to say even in the best of times, the heavier your lips feel. And sometimes there are things you can only say in the moment.

"Besides, maybe the reason Yukinon couldn't say anything was because of family stuff. Not that I know anything about that. Haruno is just scary…"

I don't think Yukinoshita was necessarily trying to cover for her family. It's true that it'd be hard to describe Yukinoshita's family environment as typical. It's not just that they were rich and locally famous—there was her sister, and I'd only gotten glimpses of her even more bizarre mother. I figured something must be going on. But, I mean, to me it's not the place of an outsider to say anything about their family affairs. "I don't really think you should intrude in their domestic problems, though."

Yuigahama *hmm*ed and pondered my comment for a bit. *"D-domestic?"* She struggled with the English word. "Oh, you mean DV!"

"Don't open your mouth when you only understand fifty percent of what you're saying. I'll punch you."

"You're gonna DV me?!"

This is not DV at all. This is just V. Visual *kei*.

"Well, just—just pretend you don't know anything about the incident or her family."

These were things Yukinoshita did not make open. Things she did not want touched should be left alone. It's not possible for people to understand one another, and pretending like you do will only make them angry.

Sometimes, indifference is welcome. Like that one time when it was raining and I was carrying a whole bunch of stuff and I slipped and fell, or when the teacher lectured me in front of the entire class... When things like that happen, you pray, *Please, let no one talk to me after this!* you know? I think it's about time everyone realized that talking to someone kindly and gently not only doesn't help, it actively causes damage. Sometimes, sympathy and compassion can be the straw that breaks the camel's back.

"Is it best to just not know, though...?" Yuigahama seemed unconvinced, hanging her head and staring at her feet. She stopped walking, so I did the same.

"I don't think ignorance is a bad thing. The more you know, the more trouble comes along with it." To have information is to undertake risk. There are plenty of things you'd be better off not knowing—a prime example being what everyone is really thinking. Everyone, to a lesser or greater extent, tricks and deceives other people. That's why the truth always hurts. The truth always shatters someone's peace.

A few seconds passed in silence. That was how long it took for Yuigahama to arrive at her own answer. "But I'd like to know more about her, you know? I want us to learn more about each other and get closer. If she's in trouble, I want to help her out." She began to walk, taking the lead. "Hikki...if Yukinon is in trouble, help her out, okay?"

"..."

I couldn't find the words to reply to that request. I could never come up with a response like Yuigahama's, not in those few seconds, not in twice that much time, or ten times that much.

I have no desire to intrude. I never have, and I never will intrude.

"Yeah, I don't think that's gonna happen," I said, encompassing many meanings at once. Yukinoshita was not going to get in trouble, she wouldn't want help from me, and I wouldn't intrude on her life.

Yuigahama looked up at the starry sky. Her sandals clacked as she kicked a pebble at her feet. "You'd still save her."

"You don't know that."

Before I could ask her what her basis was for asserting that, Yuigahama turned to look at me. "You saved me, didn't you?"

"I told you. That was just a coincidence. I didn't help you knowing it was you. So I didn't save *you* in particular." That's why even if she did feel gratitude, trust, or something more, it was all just an illusion, a misunderstanding.

If she was evaluating me based on something that anyone else—not just me—could have done, it didn't count as a positive reflection on me. Just as you can't judge someone to be a good person based on a single good act, it would bother me for someone to arbitrarily make any decision about my character based on one event. That was why Yuigahama's sentimental faith in me was all wrong. "Don't expect that kind of stuff from me."

I would surely disappoint her. That was why I wanted her to forgo any expectations from the get-go.

Yuigahama and I walked along, maintaining a fixed distance from each other. The sounds of clip-clops and dragging feet alternated through the night. The mismatched dissonance continued on, neither of us closing that small gap of a single step.

And then suddenly, the distance shrank. Yuigahama stopped suddenly, and I pitched forward, inevitably nearing her. She spun around to face me, illuminated by the soft moonlight. "Even without the accident, you still would have saved me. And I think we would have ended up going to see the fireworks together like this, too, I think."

"Of course not... There was nothing for me to save you from in the first place." In life, you don't get any what-ifs. It's all about looking back and wondering if things had been different.

But still, Yuigahama slowly shook her head. Her eyes were moist, and I could see the streetlights reflected in the corners. "No, I think there would be. I mean, it's like you said: Even if the accident hadn't happened, you would have been alone. You said the accident had nothing to do with it. And I am who I am, you know? I would have eventually had some problem, and the teacher would've taken me to the Service Club. And then I'd meet you."

Her wild speculation on what might have happened had an oddly realistic edge to it, so I couldn't easily deny or refute it. Maybe if things had begun differently, then Yuigahama, Yukinoshita, and I would have built different relationships.

As I considered this, Yuigahama continued enthusiastically. "And then you'd come up with the same kind of stupid pessimistic solution all over again. I'm sure you'd save me. And…"

I heard a sound.

Maybe it came from me, or maybe it came from her. It sounded like a gulp, or perhaps the pounding of a heart. For just one moment, she was unable to speak. Curious about what she had been about to say, I raised my head, and that's when my eyes met hers.

"And then, I just know…"

Bzz, bzz. I heard a muffled vibration. It was a phone ringing.

"Oh…" Yuigahama glanced at the drawstring coin purse in her hands but ignored her phone and attempted to continue. "I…"

"Shouldn't you answer that?" I interrupted, preventing her.

Yuigahama looked down at the coin purse she was squeezing in her hands. But that was only for a second before she pulled it out cheerfully, lifting her head with a shy *ta-ha-ha*. "…It's my mom calling. Sorry." She excused herself, took a couple of steps away, and answered the phone. "Yeah, yeah, I'm already close to home. Yeah, that's right. Huh? It's okay! You don't have to! I said I'll be home right away!" She loudly ranted about something or other before hanging up on her mom. She gave her phone a sullen glare and then returned it to the coin purse. "I live right around here, so you don't have to walk me the rest of the way. Thanks for coming this far… S-see you, then!"

"Oh…"

"Yeah, see you. Night." She gave a tiny wave good-bye.

I casually raised my hand in return. "See you, then."

Before I was even done replying, Yuigahama quickly *tap-tap-tapp*ed down the road toward her apartment. I was a little concerned that she might trip and fall on her face, but she just disappeared into a nearby apartment building, and I started walking back.

As I passed through downtown on the way home, the fervor of the festival lingered around me. Here and there I saw drunks and groups of young people hanging out and goofing around. I kept to the edge of the road to avoid them and indifferently soldiered on. With each silent step I took, the noise and tumult receded farther into the distance. Pedestrian traffic decreased, the tall buildings became sparser, and the cars were driving faster. The headlights accelerating toward me in the oncoming lane were so horribly bright, I had to stand still and look away.

But just for a moment. My averted eyes would eventually have to turn and face forward once more.

7

And as for **Hachiman Hikigaya**...

The summer was over, but only by the calendar. The final day of summer arrived, and school was starting the following day. The cicadas that announced the fall were chirping loudly, but it was still hot. It would probably be a little longer before the weather cooled.

The last sunset of August was descending. In the remaining light, I prepared for the start of school the next day. I stuffed the homework that I had finished long ago into my bag.

Among my papers was Komachi's independent research project. I had apparently gotten them jumbled together when I had printed everything I needed for submission. I flipped through the report I'd done on flame reactions one last time.

It's the flame reactions that give fireworks their color. If you touch metals or salts to a flame, each element will burn a characteristic color. Blue-white flame will also look different depending on which elements it touches.

It's actually kind of like people. When two people come in contact, you'll get some kind of reaction. And there's a range of color possibilities. Even a single person will display different reactions depending on which person they come in contact with. You create completely different colors each time, just like multicolored fireworks.

* * *

For example, when Saki Kawasaki met her, she said she was difficult to approach. Though the two girls were of the same type, and they both kept others at a distance, Kawasaki didn't feel like they could become friends. So perhaps the best form of communication for them was noninterference.

Or when Taishi Kawasaki saw her, he described her as beautiful but also scary. If you were to just skim the surface in expressing what she is, you couldn't be more accurate. Seen from afar, she may indeed be as a cliff reigning over an icy sea.

And then there was Yoshiteru Zaimokuza. When he was faced with her, he concluded that her bluntness meant she would have no reservations about hurting him. If we were only talking about that specific aspect of her, I'd say he was hitting the nail on the head. Nevertheless, I don't believe it's a question of whether she has reservations; she simply may not know any other way to be.

And then, when Saika Totsuka approached her, he called her a dignified and serious person. And that was true: She was. She is faithful to rules and principles. Though her rules and principles are based on her own internal sense of justice.

When Komachi Hikigaya came into contact with her, though, she felt that the older girl seemed somehow lonely. Both the person leaving home and the ones left behind experience the ache of solitude. Of course, Komachi's judgment was nothing more than sympathy from an outsider. Nobody knows how she really feels, probably herself included.

By contrast, Shizuka Hiratsuka watched over her, believing she was a kind person and also often righteous. Miss Hiratsuka also said the world is neither kind nor right, so it must be a difficult place for her to be. Indeed, that was true—nearly everything around her could well become her shackles. Only one thing might save her, the teacher had said: "friends." But she has most likely been tormented a dozen times more by those same "friends"—no, hundreds of times.

And Haruno Yukinoshita, who lived with her, had laughed as if to say she was worthless. With a callous smile, she commented that her little sister had always been chasing after her, and that's why she is always the loser. She is Haruno's pitiful, adorable, unchosen little sister. I don't know who it was that didn't choose her. Maybe it was friends, family, parents, or perhaps even fate. Whichever it is, only a strong person like Haruno Yukinoshita could feel sorry for her. I've never once felt that way.

But then Yui Yuigahama, having been by her side all along, cried out that she liked her. There was nothing flowery about the clumsy, tactless, frank way she had howled her feelings, but I've never heard a confession so beautiful. Even Yui Yuigahama felt a wall between her and the other girl, but that only made her want to overcome the distance all the more. She longs to help her, so strongly that she would even ask for assistance from someone like me.

And as for Hachiman Hikigaya...

Had I seen nothing at all?

Sometimes, I could indeed get a vague grasp of her actions and the psychology underlying them. But that didn't mean I understood how she feels. It's just that we were in similar positions in similar environments, so that led me to make analogies. Those analogies are nothing more than offhand approximations.

People only ever see what they want to see.

I think I was honing in on something familiar to me within her. The way she persists in her aloofness, in her own sense of justice, and doesn't lament about how misunderstood she is or how she's given up on understanding others. She unquestionably had that perfect superhuman nature I was attempting to master.

I…don't feel any desire to know more about her.

The Yukino Yukinoshita I've seen is always beautiful and honest and never lies—her brusque statements often say more than necessary. She has no one to rely on, and yet she continues to stand on her own two feet.

The way she stood there, beautiful like frozen blue flame, so ephemeral, even tragic…

That Yukino Yukinoshita…

…was the one I admired.

8

Yukino Yukinoshita stands in place, just for a moment.

August 31 and September 1: Though these days are in sequence, no other two moments in time are as clearly divided as these. There lies the boundary line between the regular and the irregular. When weekdays and weekends cross paths, that is where I wish to close the curtains on the story of Hachiman Hikigaya. The period at the end of a holiday has so much Bad Energy stored up, it's bad enough to take the whole world to the Worst Ending.

And so that day, school began again.

It had been a long time since I'd last taken my bicycle down that road to school. It was exactly the same as it was two months ago. The road was crowded, and the closer I got to the school, the unrulier the hubbub became. Everyone else must have built up lots of things to talk about over summer vacation. They were all strolling along with their friends.

As you might expect, since I had been going to this school for over a year, I saw more than a few familiar faces among them. Although their faces were the only familiar thing about them. I might catch sight of Tobe or run into Ebina, but I wouldn't talk with them, and we wouldn't greet each other.

I wouldn't really say that the summer was an illusion. It was just that camp had been a temporary, exceptional situation, and that was the only reason we had talked. There's a different sort of socializing and a different sense of distance when you're away from school. I know my place when it comes to all that.

That's why, even if I did encounter someone I knew, like Kawasaki, I would maintain my usual silence. Instead of associating with all those people patting shoulders even though they're normally not that close and asking *Did you get a tan?* even though they don't know their "friend's" former complexion, it's far sincerer to not even look at them.

There were a number of people by the school entrance who were silent like me, perhaps because they thought the same way. But when they met with people they knew, their faces would suddenly light up, and they would gleefully begin their chatter. I think the real reason they're so happy to have someone talk to them is because it fulfills their desire to be personally acknowledged. They're gloating because they're pleased to be recognized as a person, to be allowed to exist, to be approved as worth speaking to. Taken another way, it means if you are capable of acknowledging yourself, you don't need to bother with social confirmation. I would argue that a loner's isolation truly endorses his value as a person.

These ideas are what I love about myself. *Aw, good ol' Hachiman, he's so great!* I attempted to self-generate love to fulfill my desire for personal acknowledgment on my own. You could also describe it as self-poisoning via overdose. *I suppose this means I'm the one giving out love now, aren't I? I see... So I am actually... God.*

As I pondered this idiocy (society calls it philosophy), I was walking down the hallway. I had already spent half of my high school days in this school building. It had become such a familiar sight to me, but eventually, it would fade from memory.

In my clouded field of vision, I caught sight of a certain figure standing there that I surely wouldn't forget. She stood on the glass-walled staircase, and even with the sunlight streaming in and the heat rising, she radiated a frigid and awesome air that permitted no one to approach.

It was Yukino Yukinoshita.

When my foot tapped on the stairs, she noticed my presence and turned around. "Oh, it's been a while."

"Yeah. Long time no see." I was already used to having her talk down to me.

Yukinoshita ascended the stairs at the same pace as me, as if she were matching her pace to mine. So the distance between us, two steps, still remained.

"Hikigaya." She spoke to me without turning around. I replied with only a nod. It took Yukinoshita a few seconds to take my silence as a response before she continued. "So you met my sister?"

I heard her voice clearly, despite all the other students coming and going around us. "Yeah, I happened to run into her."

I wondered about my voice. I wondered if she heard me clearly. Before I could find out, the stairs ended. We had come out at the hallway leading to the second-year classrooms. To the left was Yukinoshita's Class J, and Class I. To the right were classes H to A.

At the point where we would part ways after the gap between us closed, Yukinoshita paused. "Um..."

"Is club starting up again today?" I passed her, glancing back over my shoulder at her.

She seemed at a loss, not knowing what to say for once. "Y-yes... that's the plan..."

"Roger. I'll see you then." I started walking again before I was even done. I could feel her gaze on my back. I sensed only that she was about to say something and heard the sound of a swallow. Still, I was unable to stop.

Every classroom I passed by was overflowing with energy and the joy of reunion. Class F was no exception, and nobody noticed when I entered the classroom. I was privately relieved. *Phew.* I haven't changed.

I like myself. I have never once felt like I hate myself. I do not at all hate my fundamentally high caliber, my decent looks, and my pessimistic, realistic ideas. But for the first time, I feel like I could come to hate myself.

I get these expectations, push my ideals on others, latch on to the idea that I understand someone, and then get disappointed, all in my head. I have told myself not to again and again, but even so, I have ultimately not fixed the problem.

Even Yukino Yukinoshita lies. I hate myself for being unable to allow that, even though it's so obvious.

Afterword

Hello, this is Wataru Watari.

We've finally hit summer, the perfect season for shutting yourself up at home and lying around in an air-conditioned room watching anime and reading manga. Hey, no, don't get the wrong idea. I'm just a health freak. I avoid direct sunlight and going outside in order to decrease my risk of skin cancer. It is not at all that I have no plans to go out and be social.

But seriously, you've got to be careful. They call it summer *break*, so if you don't dutifully take a break at home, you'll actually be treading treacherous waters, legally speaking.

And speaking of danger, summer is full of dangers, you know. There's the ocean, and then mountains, rivers, wealth… No, wait, that's an *enka* singer. There's an abundance of other dangers, too, you know. Pools and arcades, malls, shopping districts, commuter trains, workplaces, also workplaces, and plus, workplaces. Or even workplaces, too. Oh, and workplaces.

You see these people when you're on the commuter train—people heading to Tokyo Disneyland. You'll be on your way home, hand on one of the hanging straps as you start to nod off, and you see these couples wearing *nezumimimi* mouse ears, or *nezu-mi* for short…

Seeing them makes me think about things, you know? Like, *What the hell was I doing when I was a teenager?* or *I wonder why I'm working* or *Why do I have a job?* or *For what reason am I employed…?* You know, all kinds of things.

Recently, I've been sleeping about three hours a night on average. But since I finished the draft for Volume 5, I will be freed from that lifestyle for a while. I'm saying good-bye to that old life! Good-bye, days of only being able to sleep three hours a night! Hello, my days of only being able to sleep an hour and a half a night!

…Wait, what?

Yes, well, there are so many people who are enthusiastically shrieking with anticipation for my work… How should I put it, um, I'd like a little more sleep than that, so would someone please be my breadwinner? Any who are willing, please send a letter to the editing department of Shogakukan Gagaga Bunko. I'll be waiting.

A lot of people have expressed their concern for me, like "Oh, it must be rough!" but I love working and writing, so it's okay. Right now, I'm just being like, you know, "I—I don't like working at all! R-really, okay! I-I'm actually totally fine…"

I'll still keep working hard!

Anyway, as it was announced on the obi ad of this volume—and can you believe it—*My Youth Romantic Comedy Is Wrong, as I Expected* is being made into a TV anime! Yay! People used to tell me, like, "You won a prize, but your books are some of the worst-selling ever," or "Your sales are so bad, I can't even understand why you won a prize. Actually, what are prizes, really?" They called me Wataru Watari, Melter of Logic, the Idea General who can even destroy the idea of a book prize! But then my books got a TV anime…

It is thanks to the support of many people that I have managed to come this far. You have all taken me to a magical realm I absolutely could not have reached on my own. It's all thanks to your encouragement. Thank you so very much. Your happiness and gratitude will be my driving force as from Volume 5 and 6 and onward, I'll be stepping on the ga-ga-gas!

We've been able to see bits and pieces of a lot of things in Volume 5. Hachiman's heart has moved just a tad; his world has inched forward and taken a step backward and then spun in place just a little bit. You can see that anywhere, of course, but this is his unique story just for him. I wonder how things will go in Volume 6. I'll get help and piggyback rides and hugs from lots of people for the next volume, too! I'll work so hard to reply on a higher power, Shinran will weep tears of joy in his grave!

Below is the same old acknowledgments section.

To holy Ponkan⑧: You've been doing so much work lately, not only this volume but the extras and everything. You're doing an 8man job! Thank you for all your hard work. Finally, it's Totsuka on the cover! Yay! Thank you so much!

To my editor, Hoshino-sama: U-um… I-I'm really…sorry… No, you've got it wrong, actually, um…but if I say any more, it'll just be an excuse, so… A-anyway, thank you very much!

To Watari Wataru-sama: Thank you for your comments on the obi. They were so amazing, you would never know that it was a last-minute editorial decision to make you do it! Wait, what the heck is this?

To all the writers: As you all were just barely blasting through deadlines like *Bojack Unbound* and I was busy drinking, you came up with stories and alibis for me and worked things out with my editor and everything. Thank you so much. I'll be counting on you all next time, too.

And to all my readers: Thank you for your continuous support. Every time I get a warm comment or impression from a reader, it makes my sleepiness, my back pain, and my exhaustion all fly away. It's something of a drug. I think there's still much to come in this series, so I am blessed to have your unfaltering patronage and encouragement. Thank you very much. I hope you'll stay with me.

Now then, on that note, I think I will set down my pen here.

On a certain day in August, in a certain place in Chiba prefecture, while admonishing myself for being even sweeter to myself than MAX Coffee,

Wataru Watari

Chapter 1 … All of a sudden, the tranquility of the Hikigaya household collapses.

P. 5 ***"Why don't I smoosh your toe beans, too?!"*** This is a play on a lyric from the 1980s' heavy metal band Seikima-II. At the beginning of the song "Rouningyou no Yakara" (House of wax dolls), the lead singer yells out the line, "Why don't I turn you into a wax doll, too?"

P. 6 **"In other words, she is a woman whose future has just begun, and ultimately, she is also the last among her kin: She is the alpha and omega."** The second half of the *kanji* character for "sister" appears in the word for "future" and "youngest child."

P. 7 **"I love, love, really love, super love you, too."** *Suki Suki Daisuki Chou Aishiteru* by Outarou Maijou is not a straightforward romance story, but a thoughtful novel on the nature of love.

P. 8 **"Gazelles are only supposed to show up on the savanna, at zoos, or in *Kinnikuman Nisei*."** *Gazelleman* is the name of a character in *Kinnikuman Nisei* by Yudetamago, a sequel series to the original *Kinnikuman* comedy superhero series, also known as *Ultimate Muscle* in English.

P. 9 ***The Outer Zone*** is a science fiction manga by Shin Mitsuhara about another dimension called the Outer Zone, drawing heavily from the American science fiction TV show *The Twilight Zone*, which was known as *The Mystery Zone* in Japan.

P. 9 **"I guess I'm nothing but a rude and brash fool. I might even end up spilling ashes all over the mortuary tablet at my dad's funeral."** The legendary general of the Warring States era, Oda Nobunaga, was often referred to in these terms when he was young, and he was said to have deliberately spilled the ashes from incense on the mortuary tablet at his father's funeral.

P. 10 **"Haven't you heard? You're living in a haunted house!"** In the Studio Ghibli movie *My Neighbor Totoro*, the young boy Kanta says this to Granny and Satsuki.

P. 10 **Frisky Mon Petit** is a brand of cat food.

P. 10 The **Beast Spear**, from the manga *Ushio and Tora* by Kazuhiro Fujita, is a supernatural weapon. When used, the user transforms with it, and the transformation often involves growing a lot of long hair.

P. 10 A **spinning pile driver** is one of Zangief's special attacks, originally introduced in *Street Fighter II*.

P. 11 **"...I didn't know what to do. *Woof, woof, wa-woof.*"** This is a line from a children's song called "Inu no Mawari-san" (The doggy policeman). In the song, the policeman encounters a little kitty girl who doesn't know the way home, and he doesn't know how to help her. He just says, "Woof, woof, wa-woof."

P. 11 **"I am The Japanese That Can Say No..."** *The Japan That Can Say No* was an essay written by the politician Shintaro Ishihara in 1989.

The gist of the essay was about taking a hard line with the United States in negotiations instead of playing a yes-man to America.

P. 13 **"It's like that old saying, 'He's full of eight hundred lies.' Except with me, it's eighty thousand. 'Cause I'm Hachiman."** Hachiman's name is a pun on the number eighty thousand. In Japanese, "eight hundred lies" is an idiom meaning "full of lies."

P. 16 **"Am I a certain former spirit detective now…?"** Hachiman is referring to Shinobu Sensui, the main antagonist of the Chapter Black Saga of the *shonen* battle manga *YuYu Hakusho* by Yoshihiro Togashi. Sensui has a particular loathing for the human race.

P. 16 **"Friends, I like cats… I love every single cat that lives upon this earth."** This is a parody of a speech from the Major in *Hellsing* by Kouta Hirano. In the original speech, he is talking about how much he loves war.

P. 16 **"I hate anyone who doesn't value life!"** This is a characteristic quote from Therru in the Studio Ghibli movie *Tales from Earthsea.*

Chapter 2 … Sure enough, he's forgotten **Saki Kawasaki.**

P. 22 **"My goal for now was the Center Test."** The National Center Test for University Admissions is a standardized test used by some universities in Japan to determine admission, held once a year for two days. Those who do poorly must spend another year studying to take it again.

P. 22 **"Position the Center as target and pull the switch…"** This is a reference to episode 3 of *Neon Genesis Evangelion*. Shinji agrees to pilot the Eva but really doesn't want to do it. With a hollow look in his eyes, he does target practice, repeating, "Position target in the center and pull the switch."

P. 22 **"'Idiot! You hid the enemy with your own smoke!'"** After the target practice scene in episode 3 of *Evangelion*, Shinji goes in to battle the Angel Shamshel, and that's when Misato yells this at him in an attempt to snap him out of it.

P. 24 **"Blood Type Blue!"** In *Evangelion*, Blood Type Blue indicates that an entity is unambiguously one of the mysterious and deadly entities known as Angels.

P. 24 **"Her hair was so blue, I thought she was a Gagaga book."** Gagaga is the label that publishes this series. The spines on all the books they publish are deep blue.

P. 25 **"Make your square head round."** This is the slogan for Nichinoken, a cram school that mainly prepares elementary school students for middle school entrance examinations.

P. 27 **"TONE Coca-Cola Bottling should team up with somebody..."** Established in 1962 as Tone Beverages and later bought out by Coca-Cola, TONE Coca-Cola Bottling was previously located in Chiba, Ibaraki, and Tochigi prefectures, making many Japan-only beverages such as MAX Coffee. It has since been merged into Coca-Cola East Japan.

P. 29 **Tora no Ana** is an otaku-goods chain that sells manga, *doujinshi*, and related merchandise.

P. 29 **"From here on out, the game will belong to Stealth Hikki, yo!"** "This is Stealth Momo's time to shine!" is a quote from Momoko Touyoko in the mah-jongg manga *Saki* by Ritz Kobayashi. She calls herself "Stealth Momo" because she is so often ignored and unnoticed.

P. 29 **"Then I'd just have to put up some on-screen text to reassure everyone that **the staff ate it all afterward!*"** This line is generally an empty placation used on TV shows where they waste food in this way. Often, older viewers who remember the postwar austerity get angry when they see food wasted.

P. 29 **"I could actually feel my soul gem darkening."** In *Magical Girl Madoka Magica*, soul gems are the source of magical girls' power, and when they turn black due to emotional disturbances, the magical girl becomes a witch bent on destruction.

P. 32 **Sano Yakuyoke Daishi** is one of three temples built in worship of the Buddhist leader Ryougen, while Kawasaki Daishi is the name of one of three temples built in worship of Kuukai. Both temples are situated in the Kanto area.

P. 33 **"*Stop looking at my face. Look at my body.*"** This is a quote from *Sannen B-gumi Kinpachi-sensei* (Mr. Kinpachi from class 3-B), a TV drama about a middle school teacher and his ninth-grade class that originally began running in 1979, with multiple spin-off series running up until 2011. This particular quote is from the character Reiko Yamada, a delinquent girl, in the original 1979 run.

P. 33 **"*The Law of the High School Student*"** is a parody of the oath of the Shinsengumi, a special police force organized by the military government in 1864. The vice commander of which, Toshizou Hijikata, was known for his brutal reputation. He was the son of a wealthy farmer, and not of the samurai class (the nobility).

P. 35 **"These days, I also like to say *Know others and know thyself, and thou shalt retreat from one hundred battles.*"** The original Sun Tzu quote is, of course, "Know others and know thyself, and thou shalt not be imperiled in a hundred battles."

P. 36 **"What an open and honest opinion. I'd like to present him with a variety pack of axes."** This is in reference to Aesop's fable of the honest woodsman. The story involves a woodsman who is rewarded for his honesty with the present of a golden ax.

P. 36 **"*First, I'll destroy that screwed-up illusion of yours!*"** This is a quote from Touma Kamijo in the first volume of the light novel series *A Certain Magical Index* by Kazuma Kamachi. His magic skill is to negate other people's powers.

Chapter 3 ··· **Saika Totsuka** has surprisingly subdued tastes.

P. 43 **"Or is it getting a full-time job, or turning twenty?"** Twenty is the legal age of majority in Japan.

P. 44 **"The laws of the universe mean nothing…"** This is a quote from Exdeath, the final boss of *Final Fantasy V*. It's become a minor Internet meme, referenced whenever it seems like something incredible or disturbing might happen.

P. 44 **"When you mess with August… *Totsuka is coming!*"** In this paragraph, Hachiman is inserting bits of the catchphrases of various characters from *Smile Pretty Cure!*, released in English as *Glitter Force*.

P. 45 A **Mini 4WD** is a miniature race car that runs on a battery pack without remote control. The ones popular in Japan, sold primarily by the toy manufacturer Tamiya, are often hand assembled and highly customizable. You generally have to run them on a racetrack for them to run properly. They are mostly popular in Asia, but they're also sold in a number of other countries. There was also a tie-in manga and anime called *Bakusou Kyoudai Let's + Go!!*.

P. 46 **Medal games** are ubiquitous at Japanese arcades. They are a sort of simulated gambling, since there are no casinos in Japan (gambling is illegal). You buy medals to play the game, and the game pays out in more medals.

P. 48 **"I've touched an angel!"** "Tenshi ni Fureta yo!" (We've touched an angel!) is the name of a *K-On!* song by Ho-kago Tea Time, the voice actresses from the *K-On!* anime.

P. 49 **"The left hand is just for support!"** This is a reference to a line from the basketball manga *Slam Dunk* by Takehiko Inoue. In one scene, Akagi teaches Hanamichi Sakuragi how to shoot—he's describing holding a basketball. The quote has spawned an Internet meme, used to tag images whenever a left hand is cupping anything.

P. 49 **"The ever-obnoxious movie thief's wiggly anti-piracy dance didn't get on my nerves that day."** The movie thief (*eiga dorobou*) is an anti-piracy mascot, a man in a suit with the head of a digital camcorder who does a mime dance. In ads, he is often paired with a man in a policeman's uniform with a police light for a head. Anti-piracy ads featuring this duo are ubiquitous in Japanese movie theaters. The movie thief and movie cop have become popularized in fan art, parody videos, and even *yaoi doujinshi*.

P. 52 **"I call this stage Black RX."** A reference to *Kamen Rider: Black RX*, the ninth installment of the classic show that ran from 1988 to 1989.

P. 52 **"Was it Shinkiba? ...Well, I don't care if he's a Zaimoku or a Kimuraya or what."** Shinkiba is the name of a station in Tokyo. *Zaimoku* means "lumber" or "wood." Kimuraya is a bakery chain store. All three words have the character for "wood" in them, like Zaimokuza's name.

P. 53 **Lafcadio Hearn** (1850–1904) was an international writer best known for his books about Japan, most famously *Kwaidan: Stories and Studies of Strange Things*, about Japanese ghost stories. His Japanese pen name was Yakumo Koizumi.

P. 53 **Kyouka Izumi** (1873–1939) was a prewar novelist and playwright; much of his work features a certain supernatural element drawing on folklore and popular literature. **Kunio Yanagita** (1875–1962) was a folklorist particularly interested in local village customs and the lives of the common people, publishing a handful of books on folklore. **Shinobu Orikuchi** (1887–1953) was his disciple, a folklorist and writer.

P. 54 **"She Who Must Not Be Named is far more fearsome...*foy*."** The character Malfoy from Harry Potter is often referred to on the Internet by Japanese fans as "Foy," and it has also turned into a humorous sentence-ending particle, *foy*.

P. 55 The **Pomera** is a minimalist device purely used for notes and writing, with no apps or distractions attached. It's about the size of a tablet, but with a built-in keyboard.

P. 56 **"I'm not Inventor Boy Kanipan."** *Hatsumei Boy Kanipan* (Inventor boy Kanipan) is a 1998–1999 anime about a young boy on a planet where humans and robots live together aiming to become an inventor.

P. 57 **"And just so you know, if they bring up ED, then they're Pelé."** The former Brazilian soccer player starred in an advertisement about erectile dysfunction, which became quite popular on the Japanese Internet.

P. 57 **"They should write that he was cute in times past in *Konjaku Monogatari* and teach it in schools."** *Konjaku Monogatari* (published in English as *Japanese Tales from Times Past: Stories of Fantasy and Folklore from the Konjaku Monogatari Shu*) is a collection of stories written during the Heian period.

P. 57 **"'I had it outfitted with a real hammer. In a head-on collision, it would destroy any opponent without exception...' I also attached the marking pin from a sewing set onto my Ray Stinger."** In the *Bakusou Kyoudai Let's + Go* manga and anime series, Mini 4WD competitors often attached real weapons to their cars in order to take out their opponents. Ray Stinger in particular was outfitted with a needle.

P. 58 **"I was inches from punching the air in front of me and yelling out *Go! Maaaaagnum!* Wait, that's Galactica Magnum."** Magnum is the name of one of the two main cars in *Bakusou Kyoudai Let's + Go!* Galactica Magnum, on the other hand, is the name of a special punch in *Ring ni Kakero*, the classic boxing manga by Masami Kurumada.

P. 58 The **Avante** model Mini 4WD by Tamiya is an older "classic" model Mini 4WD originally released in the 1980s. By contrast, Beak Spider and Brocken Gigant are from the 1990s.

Chapter 4 ··· Unfortunately, nobody knows where **Shizuka Hiratsuka**'s red thread went.

P. 64 **"A *real* stay-at-home wife hands her husband a five-hundred-yen coin for his lunch..."** Traditionally speaking, the wife handles the family finances in a Japanese household. The husband hands her his paycheck, and she handles the bills and gives him an allowance.

P. 64 **"I'm a full-wallet alchemist."** The original Japanese here was *kogane no renkinjutsushi*, meaning "pocket change alchemist," in reference to the manga by Hiromu Arakawa, *Hagane no Renkinjutsushi* (*Fullmetal Alchemist*).

P. 64 **Takeoka-style ramen** is a type of shoyu ramen where the base is boiled with the Japanese variant on *char siu* (barbecue pork). **Katsuura *tantanmen*** is a slight variation on the Szechuan *dan-dan* noodles, a spicy noodle bowl with minced pork.

P. 65 **"I was not preoccupied with a single spot. I saw everything in its entirety…effortlessly. That is what it means to truly 'see,' or so I hear."** This is a quote from the manga *Vagabond* by Takehiko Inoue.

P. 66 **"Drop dead, amen…"** This is from the lyrics of the song "Wedding Bell" by Sugar, a song where a woman is resentful about a man and a woman getting married.

P. 66 **"The spiritual pressure…disappeared…?"** This line is repeated over and over in *Bleach* by Tite Kubo, especially in reference to Chad. Among Japanese fans on the Internet, it has been shorthand to describe someone dying or being knocked out.

P. 68 **"Ramen! Do people do that?"** This is a reference to a line from *Kodoku no Gurume* (The lonely gourmet) by Masayuki Qusumi and Jiro Taniguchi. The original line is "Takeaway! Do people do that?" when he sees a man taking pork miso soup as takeaway. He thinks since it will get cold, it won't be any good.

P. 68 **"Does she have a full ABCD encirclement going on here?"** ABCD encirclement was the Japanese name for foreign nations against Japan in the 1940s, including America, Britain, China, and the Dutch.

P. 69 **"…I would whirl them around, call the move *Tsubame Gaeshi*, and then tell everyone it was a family trade secret."** *Tsubame*

Gaeshi, meaning literally "swallow's return," or sometimes "turning swallow cut," was originally a move invented by the famous swordsman Kojirou Sasaki. The term has since been used to describe a variety of martial arts moves, both real and fictitious, from a real judo move to a special attack in *Fate stay/night* to a tennis strike in *Prince of Tennis*.

P. 74 **"Unfortunately, I'm more into the future boy than the boy detective."** *Detective Conan*, known as *Case Closed* in North America, is an extremely long-running and popular manga by Gosho Aoyama that began running in 1994. It's about a high school detective trapped in the body of a child. *Future Boy Conan* is much older—it's a 1978 TV postapocalyptic science fiction anime directed by Hayao Miyazaki. The two Conans are totally unrelated; they just have the same name.

P. 77 **"...with the texture of a flounder dancing on your tongue."** In the Japanese, Hikigaya says *shakkiripon*, a made-up word from the manga *Kodoku no Gurume* (The lonely gourmet). The word is supposed to mean "the texture of a flounder dancing on your tongue."

P. 78 ***Kyuuri*** means "cucumber," which sounds somewhat like the name Kiryuu. Kiryuu Bannenchiten is a character from the harem manga *Mamotte Shugogetten* (Protect me, Shugogetten) that ran from 1997 to 2000.

P. 78 **Pepsi Ice Cucumber** was a short-lived Japan-only product that was distributed in 2007 and cancelled the same year.

P. 81 ***Iekei* ramen** is the name of a style of ramen with *tonkotsu* soy sauce base and thick straight noodles, originating with the shop Yoshimuraya in 1974. Ramen shops that serve this kind of ramen generally append *ya* at the end of their names, like Yoshimuraya.

P. 81 **"When you take the *meat* radical and add *delicious* to it, you get *fat.*"** Miss Hiratsuka is talking about the shape of the Chinese characters. 月 (meat) plus 旨(delicious) equals 脂 (fat).

Chapter 5 ... **Komachi Hikigaya** considers that one day, her brother may leave.

P. 83 **"Bancho Sarayashiki"** is a classic ghost story. While there are a number of variations on the tale, all versions of the story involve the ghost of a woman counting plates and always coming up one short.

P. 83 **"If I put a circle on the calendar, that would be *Takoyaki Manto Man.*"** "Karendaa ni Maru" (Circle on the calendar) is the name of the ending theme song of *Takyoyaki Manto Man* (Octopus ball Cape Man), an anime about *takoyaki* fighting crime.

P. 83 **"Hey, did you do a time leap?"** This is a reference to *The Girl Who Leapt Through Time*, a novel by Yasutaka Tsutsui that was originally published in installments from 1965 to 1966. It has been adapted many times, most famously into the 2006 animated film directed by Mamoru Hosoda.

P. 85 **"Kamakura snorted a *funsu!* and stood from where he was sprawled over my feet."** *Funsu!* is the characteristic snorting noise that Yui Hirasawa from *K-On!* makes when she's getting fired up. It originally appeared in the sixth episode of the anime.

P. 85 The **catbus** from the movie *My Neighbor Totoro* has an especially large mouth.

P. 86 **"I promptly began howling toward the future."** "Mirai e no Houkou" (Howling toward the future) is the name of a song by JAM Project, which featured in the H game *Muv-Love Alternative.*

P. 87 **"Why do the fireflies die so quickly?"** This is a quote from Setsuko in the movie *Grave of the Fireflies*, foreshadowing her and her brother's death. In the Japanese, her Kansai accent makes this line all the more iconic.

P. 87 **"...*Oh, this reminds me of the Showa era!*"** The Showa era spanned the years 1926 to 1989, corresponding with the reign of the Showa emperor, Hirohito. The current era is the Heisei, beginning when Akihito ascended to the throne.

P. 88 **"It's like how you'll learn moves faster if you cancel evolution with the B button."** Hachiman is referring to, of course, evolving Pokémon.

P. 88 **"Komachi and I stopped, waiting there for Sablé to finish literally chewing the scenery."** The original Japanese is "Sablé was literally eating grass by the roadside," a Japanese idiom that means "wasting time."

P. 89 **"...but if some random hippo suddenly showed up to greet me and recommend me some mouthwash, I would not feel blessed at all."** This is a reference to a 1995 ad for an Isodine (*isojin*), a gargling solution to prevent sickness. A woman comes home, saying, "There's no one here to welcome me home..." and she's greeted by a couple of miniature hippos (mascots for the brand), and they gargle together.

P. 91 **"What is this loneliness you speak of? Is it something you'll go check out, something you'll go find in your neighborhood Akihabara?"** Hachiman is referencing a 1990s ad for the Sato Musen electronics company (merged with Yamada Denki in 2008). The ad features a pair of leopards (the company logo featured a leopard) riding skateboards and enticing the viewer to come check out, come find a wonderful something in your neighborhood Akihabara. They use the English word *something*, which Hachiman is trying to rhyme here with *samishii* (lonely).

P. 92 **"I'll stay at home until I get married off... Then until I get married on."** Japanese has a number of different words for "marriage" that are gender specific. *Totsugu*, the first word he used, is for women, as she leaves her family to become a housewife in her husband's family. *Mukogu* is a made-up word from the word *muko*, meaning "son-in-law," and references the practice of *mukoiri*, in which a man with no sons adopts his daughter's husband as his heir instead, and the son-in-law adopts his new father's surname. This is fairly rare, but it does happen on occasion.

P. 95 ***"They're so good, they could even work on the Ant King."*** The Chimera Ant King is the antagonist of one of the later arcs of the manga *Hunter x Hunter* by Yoshihiro Togashi.

P. 97 The **Siege of Osaka** was a series of battles near the end of the Sengoku era undertaken by the Tokugawa shogunate against the Toyotomi clan—Tokugawa won. Osaka Castle had two moats around it.

P. 98 **"Sheeeh!"** is a comic pose that originated from the character Iyami in the classic manga *Osomatsu-kun* by Fujio Akatsuka. The pose became something of a fad in the 1960s and onward.

P. 98 **Ray Sefo** is a New Zealand kickboxer, boxer, and mixed martial artist, famous for letting his guard down to taunt his opponent, telling him to go ahead and take a shot.

P. 99 **"Itchy. Tasty."** is a famous line from a journal in the original *Resident Evil* game. The journal describes an animal keeper slowly becoming infected with the zombie virus and losing his mind. The only thing written on the very last page is *Itchy. Tasty.*

Chapter 6 … And so **Yui Yuigahama** disappears into the throng.

P. 106 Hamtaro is the protagonist of a children's manga and storybook series of the same name by Ritsuko Kawai, with a very popular anime adaptation. He's a hamster.

P. 106 "*The only thing I can think of that's this silent is Seagal.*" In Japanese ads for the movies starring the old action star Steven Seagal, his character was often described as "The silent _____."

P. 110 Kabaya is a Japanese confectionery company. They have a line of products called "Ju-C."

P. 111 Toei Animation is one of the most famous and successful animation studios in Japan, producing many hit long-running series that are popular with small children, such as the franchises of Dragon Ball, One Piece, and Pretty Cure. Their parent company, a film and television corporation, also does live-action *sentai* series such as *Kamen Rider*. These series in particular are often featured on cotton candy bags to appeal to children.

P. 112 *Jewelpet Pretty Cure* is a crossover series between Pretty Cure and the Jewelpet franchise, and *Pretty Rhythm* is an arcade game based off *Pretty Cure*. Both are rather obscure spin-offs of what is a massive, sprawling franchise marketed at little girls. As with any magical girl show, though, there is an adult male following.

P. 112 *Tokumei Research 200X* was an old TV variety show that ran from 1996 to 2004. It mainly focused on occult topics.

P. 112 "I'll become a tree!" This is a reference to a line from the character Eru Chitanda from the Kotenbu series of mystery novels by Honobu

Yonezawa, which was adapted into the anime *Hyouka*. She has the habit of saying "*Watashi, ki ni narimasu!*" ("I'm curious!"). Hachiman has punned this (as this line so often is), reading the line as "I'll become a tree!" by changing the kanji for *ki* to mean "tree."

P. 113 "Why are you making it sound like the *All-Girls Swimming Show*?" Yuigahama is talking about *Doki! Marugoto Mizugi! Onna Darake no Suiei Taikai* (Heart pounding! All swimsuits! The all-girls swimming show!), a spin-off of the *Swimming Show* idol pop star variety show that began in 1970, with swimming as a theme. 1988 was the first season of the all-girls edition, which continued until 2003.

P. 117 "It's a habit of mine to walk without making a sound." This is a quote from the character Killua in the long-running *shonen* manga *Hunter X Hunter* by Yoshihiro Togashi. Killua was trained from birth to be an assassin.

P. 117 "...like I was dodging wooden men to become a Shaolin monk..." *Shaolin Wooden Men* (1976) is a Jackie Chan film. The scene Hachiman refers to is the graduation ceremony of Shaolin monks, which involves passing through a corridor while dodging kicks and punches from wooden men all along the way.

P. 120 "She tugged my ear just like Sazae does to Katsuo." The classic manga *Sazae-san* began its run in 1946 in a regional newspaper, finally ending in 1974. The anime series began in 1969 and continues to this day, making it the longest-running animated series of all time, beating out even *Doraemon*. It's essentially a domestic comedy about a housewife, Sazae-san, and her family. Katsuo is her younger brother—over ten years younger than Sazae—and she often grabs him by the ear like that. Nakajima is Katsuo's best friend, and Katsuo often invites him to go play baseball.

P. 120 **"I am not playing the field... It's not gonna happen."** The original text here was something to the effect of "Playing around? Getting serious? No way would that ever happen. That's about as implausible as *Motivation! Energy! Iwaki!* I don't know what she wanted me to say, but it can't be anything good-*zaki*!" In Japanese, it's a series of words ending in the syllable *ki*. First is *uwaki* (cheating/playing around) and *honki* (serious). Then it's followed by a play on the campaign slogan for the former LDP member Nobuko Iwaki: *Yaruki, genki, Iwaki!* (Motivation, energy, Iwaki!). Finally, he references a phrase from a political ad for Takenori Kanzaki, *Sou wa Ikanzaki!* (That's Ikanzaki!), which itself puns on the phrase *Sou wa ikan zo!* (We can't have that!)

P. 121 **"There were so many *dodonpas*, I was like, are you Mercenary Tao or what?"** In Akira Toriyama's manga *Dragon Ball*, Mercenary Tao is the first character featured using the skill Dodonpa, which is sometimes translated as "Dodon Ray" or occasionally "Boom Wave."

P. 123 **"That's beyond a fortified armor shell; that's basically a Gundam."** A "fortified armor shell" is the name of the mecha suit from the manga *Apocalypse Zero* by Takayuki Yamaguchi. It's small and fits the human body—about the size of an Iron Man suit. A mobile suit from the Gundam franchise is far larger—giant-robot sized.

P. 127 **"Yep, this sauce is indeed a boy flavor."** This is a reference to a line from the manga *Kodoku no Gurume* (The lonely gourmet).

Chapter 8 ... **Yukino Yukinoshita** stands in place, just for a moment.

P. 143 **"When weekdays and weekends cross paths, that is where I wish to close the curtains on the story of Hachiman Hikigaya."** This is a play on the tagline from the *A Certain Magical Index* series by

Kazuma Kamachi, the original being "When science and magic cross paths, a story is born."

P. 143 "The period at the end of a holiday has so much Bad Energy stored up, it's bad enough to take the whole world to the Worst Ending." This is a reference to the main conflict of *Smile Pretty Cure*, the ninth installment of the Pretty Cure franchise. The villains are from a place called Bad End Kingdom. They travel to earth to collect Bad Energy to inflict the Worst Ending on all the worlds in the universe.

Afterword

P. 149 "There's the ocean, and then mountains, rivers, wealth... No, wait, that's an *enka* singer." Yamakawa Yutaka is an *enka* singer whose name is spelled with the characters for "mountain," "river," and "wealth." *Enka* is a genre of Japanese music favored by older generations that stylistically resembles traditional Japanese music.

P. 151 "I'll work so hard to reply on a higher power, Shinran will weep tears of joy in his grave!" Shinran (AD 1173–1263) was a Buddhist monk and the founder of the Joudo Shinshuu sect of Buddhism. This school preaches reliance on another power, that is to say relying on the Amitabha Buddha, rather than engaging in specific acts.

P. 151 "As you all were just barely blasting through deadlines like *Bojack Unbound*..." He is referencing the ninth *Dragon Ball Z* movie, *Bojack Unbound*. The first part of the Japanese title, *Ginga Girigiri*, means "galaxy at the brink," and in this case, they were at the brink of their deadlines.

A Loner's Worst Nightmare: Human Interaction!

MY YOUTH R♥MANTIC COMEDY iS WRØNG, AS I EXPECTED

Check out the manga too!

Hachiman Hikigaya is a cynic. He believes "youth" is a crock—a sucker's game, an illusion woven from failure and hypocrisy. But when he turns in an essay for a school assignment espousing this view, he's sentenced to work in the Service Club, an organization dedicated to helping students with problems! Worse, the only other member of the club is the haughty Yukino Yukinoshita, a girl with beauty, brains, and the personality of a garbage fire. How will Hachiman the Cynic cope with a job that requires—*gasp!*—social skills?